The Long Day Done

Jeremy Rowan Robinson

HAYLOFT

First published 2003

Hayloft Publishing, Kirkby Stephen,
Cumbria, CA17 4EU.

tel: (017683) 42300
fax. (017683) 41568
e-mail: dawn@hayloft.org.uk
web: www.hayloft.org.uk

© 2003 Jeremy Rowan Robinson

ISBN 1 904524 03 6

A catalogue record for this book is available
from the British Library

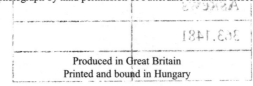

Cover photograph by kind permission of Patterdale Mountain Rescue Team

Produced in Great Britain
Printed and bound in Hungary

"So be my passing!
My task accomplished and the long day done,
My wages taken, and in my heart
Some late lark singing,
Let me be gathered to the quiet west,
The sundown splendid and serene,
Death."

From *I. M. Margaritae Sorori* by A. E. Henley

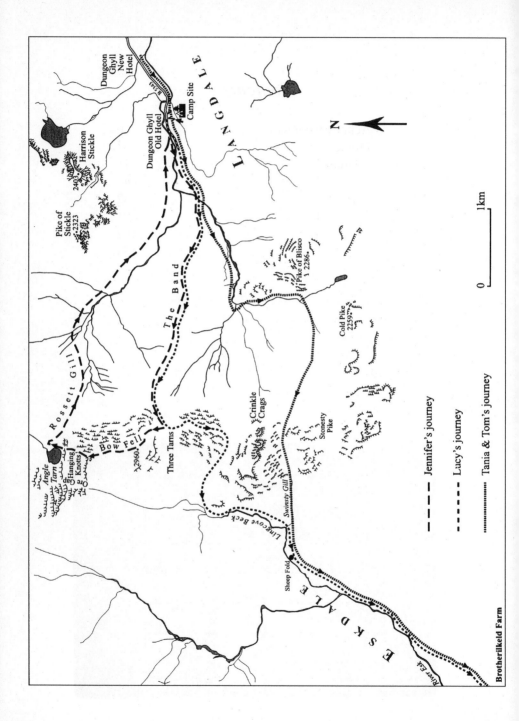

Contents

Acknowledgments

This is a work of fiction. My thesaurus offers 'fantasy' or 'cock-and-bull story' as alternatives to the word 'fiction', but I hope neither is a reflection of what I have written. I use the word to emphasise that the actual incidents described in the book did not happen and that the mountain rescue teams portrayed do not exist. I apologise to the Ambleside/Langdale and Eskdale Mountain Rescue Teams, in whose areas this story is set, if this gives rise to any confusion.

That is the extent of the fiction. Sadly, incidents of the sort described will be all too familiar to those involved in mountain rescue; and the operational aspects of the rescues are as realistic as I can make them. The book is in a sense an anatomy of a mountain rescue.

In writing it, I have received help from a number of people and am pleased to have an opportunity to acknowledge this. I particularly wish to thank my father for his guidance and support, Dick Tough of the Lomond Mountain Rescue Team for help with mountain rescue practice and procedure, Dr. David Syme for guidance on the treatment of hypothermia, Chris Cane for technical advice about flying helicopters in poor conditions, Wendy Buchan and Mark Perryman for comments on the narrative, Alison Sandison for drawing the map and my wife, Yvonne, for her insistence on the use of plain English.

This book is dedicated to the members of the mountain rescue teams throughout the UK who voluntarily give up their time to go out into the mountains at all hours of the day and night, sometimes in appalling weather, to help those in difficulties.

Jeremy Rowan Robinson
Aberdeen
September 2002

Preface

An inquest is more than a fact-finding process. It sets out to establish the cause of death; it also offers a sort of catharsis to those most closely involved, an outlet for the emotion that has built up during and immediately after the drama of a sudden and sometimes violent death.

In this case, however, the inquest seems likely to be more than that. The media interest aroused by the events of the New Year weekend in the Lakeland fells has been such that the venue has been switched from the magistrates court in Windermere to a conference hall in a nearby hotel in order to cater for the numbers expected to attend. The interest had initially been aroused by a column in one of the local papers. The column by a local journalist had questioned the wisdom of some of the decisions made during the course of difficult and drawn out mountain rescues over that weekend. The letter had provoked a furious response from some of those involved in the rescues. In the meantime, however, the matter had been taken up in an editorial in one of the tabloids:

"The events of the New Year weekend in the Lakeland fells must surely reinforce the argument in favour of full time, paid, professional mountain rescue teams such as exist in a number of European countries. We do not for one moment suggest that anyone was negligent or that the dedicated men and women involved in the rescues did other than their very best in difficult circumstances. We pride ourselves in this country on the voluntary approach to mountain rescue and it has served us well. But times are changing. Already, a great many rescues are undertaken by full time, professionally trained helicopter crews. In the light of the circumstances surrounding the events of that weekend, the question must be asked whether it is fair to put volunteers in the position of having to make life and death decisions. Over that weekend, people died, others were injured and others still were put in danger. Is it not time to go all the way and invest in full time, paid professionals to complement the helicopter crews?

A professional service need not be a burden on the tax-payer. It could be paid for through a compulsory insurance scheme. Again, we can learn from other countries here. People taking to the hills could be required to

8

take out insurance. In return, they could be confident that a well equipped, well trained, professional service would be on call to assist them if and when they get into trouble."

There was nothing very new about the argument for a professional rescue service, nor about the case for insurance. However, by linking it to the rescues over the New Year weekend, the innuendo, although carefully understated, seemed to be that the rescue teams had made mistakes or had been out of their depth. The emphasis in the editorial on a well-equipped, well-trained professional service implied that the voluntary service was neither. In the absence of other domestic news, the story was taken up more widely in the media. Again, the focus was on the argument for a professional service but the implication was that the events of the weekend demonstrated why this was required.

As a result of the media coverage, relatives of those who died began to question whether the right decisions had been made during the rescues. This, in turn, prompted the Coroner to hold an inquest into the deaths and it was reported that the relatives had retained professional representation. It began to look increasingly as though the inquest would be used by the media, if not by the Coroner, as an opportunity to investigate the conduct of the rescues on the night of 31st December and the morning of 1st January.

As a consequence, some two weeks after the rescues, David Wynn found himself lunching with one of his partners at the Hot Pot in Bowness. David had been approached that morning by the team leaders of the two rescue teams involved and asked whether he would represent them at the inquest. He was a partner in a small firm of solicitors in Windermere. He was also a member of one of the rescue teams; indeed, he had taken part in the rescues - hence the request. However, his involvement in the rescues meant that he was too closely involved to be able to represent the teams. With the agreement of the team leaders, he had therefore persuaded Gordon Penman, one of his partners and an experienced advocate, to act for them instead. The lunch was in the way of a briefing session.

The Hot Pot in Bowness is tucked away out of sight of the main road and tends to be quiet, particularly in January. Gordon and David settled themselves at a table with a view out over the Lake Windermere towards Belle Isle. It was a grey winter's day and the lake was very still, almost like a mirror, with one or two boats in view lying idly at their moorings. The island too looked grey, the trees standing bare and sparse. It was difficult to associate the view with the colourful, bustling, noisy, teaming water front of July and August.

"So tell me what happened?" asked Gordon.

David explained to Gordon that he could speak about many of the events from his own direct knowledge. Others had only became clear to him when speaking afterwards to other team members. Others still had emerged from newspaper reports. David was quiet for a moment as he assembled them in his mind in chronological order.

The events in question had begun for him on the afternoon of Friday the 30th December, although he compressed this part of the story for Gordon's benefit. He had been climbing with a friend in the Langdale valley. Eric Burns, a friend from university, had phoned in early December to say that he could get away for a few days after Christmas if he, David, wanted to show off his skills in winter climbing. That was a reference to the snow and ice-climbing course that David had attended at the mountaineering centre at Glenmore Lodge in the Cairngorms the previous winter. As November and the early part of December had been the coldest the Lake District had experienced for some years with several falls of snow, David thought there was a reasonable prospect of a bit of winter climbing at New Year. In response to Eric's call, he was able to arrange leave between Christmas and New Year.

Although David lived in Windermere, they had decided to camp at the National Trust camp site in Langdale to avoid the driving. They had brought all their snow and ice climbing gear with them; but, as so often happens in the Lake District, a few days of mixed weather meant that winter conditions were not as good as they had hoped and they had ended up doing quite a lot of walking instead. Indeed, the weather on the day this all started had been so warm and clear that they had dug out their rock climbing gear instead.

CHAPTER 1

Gimmer Crag, 3pm, Friday, 30th December

A modern climbing rope has to conform to certain standards. Its performance is measured largely by its capacity to absorb the energy of a fall through its elasticity. Too little elasticity and it becomes difficult for the second person on the rope to control a falling leader; the load on belays may become too high with increased risk of failure; the force transmitted to the falling climber may be such as to cause injury; and conceivably the rope could break.

Considerations of elasticity were not in the forefront of Eric's mind as he fell. Physics had never been his strong point. It, nonetheless, had a bearing on the consequence of the fall. Eric and David had been climbing Gimmer Crack. The route is rated very severe (mild) in the guide book and is described as "a first rate climb, comfortably old-fashioned and quite definitely one of the classic routes of the Langdale Valley." Not far from the top of the climb Eric's boots had parted company with a narrow, sloping foothold which had turned out to be icy; hardly surprising in late December. His right hand at that point in time had been groping unsuccessfully for a hold which the guide book assured him existed on the seemingly blank rock face. He was therefore left suspended for one brief, despairing moment by his left hand and just had time to say a resigned, "Oh shit" before that, too, had slipped on the cold rock and he had become airborne.

To protect himself in the event of a fall, Eric had secured a couple of running belays, or 'runners', to the rock face as he had climbed from the selection of iron-mongery attached to his harness and had looped the climbing rope through snap links attached to the runners. It was the runners rather than the rope that worried him as he parted company with the rock - and with some justification. The top runner, in the form of a metal wedge lodged in a crack, had not bedded in securely and was pulled from the crack with an explosive scraping noise by the force of the fall. One part of his mind was numb with the absolute horror at what was happening to him; but another part found time to note the failure of the runner and to put in a quick plea to the Almighty on behalf of the remaining one. In the meantime, he plunged on down the cliff with a clatter of iron-mongery and the awful noise of windproof clothing glancing off rock.

David was some 25 metres below at the other end of the rope. He was anchored to the cliff by two static belays, one a sling looped over a spike of rock, the other a small metal wedge jammed in a crack. He had been controlling the paying out of the rope with a belaying device attached to his harness, appropriately nick-named an 'air traffic controller.' He was perhaps more relaxed than he should have been and was enjoying the last of the afternoon sun when he got his first intimation of air traffic. As Eric's weight came on the runners, the limited slack in the rope was taken up at frightening speed and this was coupled almost immediately, as the second runner held and the belaying device took effect, with a vicious and powerful upward jerk on the rope. The device did not immediately stop the fall and, although David was wearing gloves, the force of the rope running through his hands caused painful rope burns and the upward jerk of the rope lifted him bodily from the ledge along with the sling looped over the spike of rock and left him anchored to the stance only by the small metal wedge. This in turn was wrenched upwards towards a wider part of the crack and threatened to pop out leaving both of them relying solely on Eric's second runner for their continued association with the cliff.

Normally, the view of the Langdale Valley looking out from Gimmer Crag is one of the finest in this part of the Lake District and this after-noon it was particularly clear. The crag is perched up above the Mickleden valley at the western end of Great Langdale. To the west the edge of Rossett Pike is visible. To the left of that is the track up Rossett Gill to Angle Tarn and Styhead Pass with access to Wasdale and Borrowdale. All that could be seen from Gimmer at this time of the day was a dark gash on the hillside. Beyond and to the south of the Gill, Bowfell and Crinkle Crags, covered in snow following the heavy and repeated falls in this unusually cold winter, stood dark in the shadows of the late afternoon. Crinkle Crags were partly masked by the Band, a prominent ridge that descends into the Langdale Valley from Bowfell. Opposite and to the south, Pike O'Blisco still caught the last of the sun that had tempted them onto the cliff.

Both of them were oblivious to all this. Eric's fall had eventually been arrested about 3 metres above David and as he hung helplessly at one end of the rope he was having difficulty in focusing on anything. Although he had benefited from the elasticity of the rope, he had nonetheless endured a significant impact force. This was because the failure of his first runner meant that he had fallen a considerable distance and the breath had been driven forcefully from his body when the rope had eventually taken the strain, elasticity notwithstanding. He was also feeling severely bruised and shaken by his contact with the rock on the way down. David recalled that some climbing texts extolled the virtues of free fall over slide or bounce in the event of a fall - not that there was usually any choice in the matter. For his part, David was hanging uncomfortably in his harness from the other end of the rope just above the ledge as a sort of counterweight and was also feeling a bit shaken and sore.

"Jesus! Are you OK?" he gasped.

It was all Eric could do to respond with a cross between a grunt and a groan. David took the response as a good sign.

Meanwhile, David was looking around urgently for somewhere to place additional protection in case Eric's remaining runner gave way and with some difficulty he managed to get a wedge into a crack and attach himself to it. Having done that, he then contrived to lower Eric the remaining ten feet to the ledge by easing the climbing rope through his belaying device. This was not easy because he was, himself, still in a state of suspension. With the weight off the rope, he was then able to sort himself out and join Eric on the ledge where he busied himself making them both secure.

"Are you OK?" repeated David. Eric was sitting hunched up on the ledge feeling shocked and sore and not inclined to talk.

"That really gave me a fright," he continued seemingly determined to hold a conversation. He was not by nature garrulous, but he had been badly shaken by the consequences of his carelessness that had nearly meant the end for both of them. Although falls are an occupational hazard with climbing and although runners sometimes fail, static belays, anchoring the person holding the rope to the cliff, should not. But for Eric's second runner, they would both have come to grief. David's stance on the ledge had been well protected against the downward pull from a fall by the second person on the rope but not against the upward pull from a falling leader. He had failed to adjust the belays when he had taken over from Eric on the stance so that they could counter a pull in either direction.

Eric, who seemed to be oblivious to how close they had come to disaster, said tentatively that he thought he was OK. Although bruised and sore from contact with the rock on the way down and still shaking from the experience, nothing was obviously broken.

"What happened?" asked David, "The first thing I knew, you were airborne."

Eric explained that his boots had slipped on some ice. "I'm afraid there wasn't time to shout a warning."

Having ascertained that he was still in one piece, he gingerly shrugged off his sack and rummaged in it for his thermos flask. It had survived the fall less well than he had; contact with the rock had cracked it in several places and coffee had leaked over everything. While he slowly emptied the sack and drained out the coffee, David reached for his and took out his flask.

"Coffee?" he asked, unscrewing the top.

"Thanks."

David got out some chocolate and broke it in two, passing one piece to Eric. Meanwhile, David was beginning to take stock of their position. Gimmer Crack is in the centre of the north west face of the crag with hard climbs on either side. It would be difficult from their present position to traverse off the route onto easier ground. They were faced with the choice of completing the climb or retreating.

"We can go up or down," he said. "Which do you want to do? I was always told that if you fall off a horse, you should immediately get back into the saddle and carry on," he added.

"Yes, well the only time I ever went riding, the horse and I parted company in a bruising fashion and I have never been anywhere near one since. I prefer my recreational interests not to have large teeth and a mind of their own," Eric observed shortly. "I know hard climbers don't think a climb is serious unless they have fallen off it several times on the way up. But I am just an ordinary mortal and I think I have had enough for today. Do you want to lead?"

David looked up the crack towards the overhang near the top of the climb. What had seemed dry and inviting no more than ten minutes ago, now looked cold and treacherous.

"No, but then there are economic considerations," he said. If they retreated, they might have to leave the runner and the snap link which had held them during the fall. They might also have to sacrifice one or two more belay slings in abseiling off the cliff. The ledge on which they were sitting was about two thirds of the way up the climb which would mean fixing at least two abseils. The bottom pitch was little more than a scramble and they could easily reverse that unroped. But the loss of that much equipment was not to be taken lightly.

"How is the runner fixed?" asked David. "Is there any chance we could try and flick it off with the rope?"

"No, it's fixed round a chock stone in the crack."

"Oh, well; that's that," he said philosophically. "Let's set up an abseil."

They pulled the climbing rope through the runner, regretfully leaving the latter in place to be collected by the next party up the Crack. Then they set up a belay for the abseil. The spike of rock to which David had been belayed seemed a solid part of the cliff and offered good security against the downward pull of an abseil and the prospect of recovering the belay at the end. David dropped a sling over the spike, passed the climbing rope through it and then dropped both ends of the rope down the cliff. Eric then clipped on to the doubled rope and, facing into the cliff, leaned backwards letting the belay take the strain and eased himself off the ledge onto the face. Then he simply walked backwards down the face aiming for a grassy ledge about 20 metres below. Arriving there, he rigged up a belay using a prominent pedestal of rock, unclipped from the rope and then shouted up that he was secure. David abseiled down to join him.

There then followed a frustrating twenty minutes while they took it in turns to try and flick their belay off the spike of rock by sending a ripple up the rope. David eventually succeeded but only after climbing up some feet from the corner of the ledge and flicking the rope from an angle. For the next belay, they decided not to risk sacrificing a sling and simply dropped the mid point of the rope over the prominent rock pedestal and dropped both ends over the edge. While David watched to see that the rope showed no inclination to work its way up the pedestal, Eric abseiled the last stretch down to easier ground. David followed and they recovered the rope by the simple expedient of pulling on one end. After coiling it, they climbed down the bottom section of the route to the scree.

Because Eric was still feeling a bit shaken, they did not stop there but set off along the ill-defined track which works its way steeply down to join the path along the Mickleden valley. Much of the light covering of snow from the night before had melted in the morning sunshine. What was left was still soft underfoot. However, a warm morning had turned into a cold afternoon and, with the sun now well behind the mountains to the west, there was promise of a heavy frost.

The path emerges at the Old Dungeon Ghyll Hotel and they arrived with the last of the daylight and made their way to the Hikers' Bar. The Old Dungeon Ghyll Hotel lacks the historic glamour of the Wasdale Head Hotel in Wasdale which was the home of early Lakeland climbing from the 1880s. The Langdale Valley did not really come into its own as a climbing centre until the first part of the twentieth century; but it has been popular ever since with Gimmer Crag, Bowfell Buttress and Pavey Ark attracting early attention, followed by White Ghyll and eventually in the 1950s Raven Crag behind the hotel itself. The guide book suggests that the proximity of the hotel bar was an important factor in developments on Raven Crag. The accessibility of the Langdale Valley to traffic pouring up from the south via the A591 to Ambleside has reinforced its popularity as one of England's premier centres for climbing and walking. The circle of hills from the Langdale Pikes to the north, Bowfell and the Crinkle Crags to the west and Pike O'Blisco to the south are household names. So, too, are Scafell Pike and Scafell which are accessible from the Valley via Rossett Ghyll and Great End.

What it lacks in glamour, the Old Hotel, or the ODG as it is generally referred to, makes up in character. It lies in a magnificent setting at the western end of Great Langdale at the point where the road from Ambleside and Chapel Stile meets the single track road coming over from Little Langdale. It nestles below Raven Crag on the north side of the valley with Harrison Stickle, the highest of the Langdale Pikes, rising behind it to 2,403 feet. It is a substantial stone and slate building which was originally a farmhouse and subsequently an inn. One way or another it has been providing a welcome to travellers for more than 300 years. The hotel is cosy with solid furniture, an open fire in the residents' lounge and something of a Victorian atmosphere.

The Hikers' Bar to which they retreated was at the side of the hotel. It was originally a cow byre and two of the stalls are still in place. On one wall hangs a large and somewhat discouraging picture of a falling climber being gathered in by the angels. It has been there as long as any-one can remember. More importantly that afternoon, there was a wel-coming open fire, part of an ancient oven. The bar was still relatively quiet. An elderly couple in walking gear sat talking by the fire. A group of young men and women were in the middle of a noisy game of darts. They, too, appeared to have come in off the hills. Jackets and rucksacks were piled on the benches and their boots were wet. David settled Eric into a seat and solicitously ordered two pints of real ale.

The beer was welcome. "If it takes a fall to get you to buy a round," said Eric, "I shall have to consider a small tactical fall at the end of every route."

"If that was a small tactical fall, I hope I'm not around when you have a serious one," David retorted smiling.

Eric and David had known each other for about ten years. They had been law students together at university in West Yorkshire and had joined the university mountaineering club at the same time. As new members, and from the same department, they had drifted together and, after a while, had discovered that they suited each other as climbing partners. Neither was particularly gregarious. They didn't dislike company and were perfectly capable of holding their end up in a group; but they did-n't seek company. Eric was quiet, had a good sense of humour and appeared self contained and confident. David had enjoyed Eric's combi-nation of enthusiasm and caution and his commitment to doing rather than talking. The club had had its fair share of armchair mountaineers. What Eric saw in him he was not sure.

Although they had both done a lot of hill walking, they had only start-ed rock climbing at university. Physically they were opposites. Eric was tall and lean, well over six feet, which is an asset when leading a climb. His tendency to stoop and his full beard, which he kept well trimmed, made him look older than his 29 years. In contrast, David was short, a modest five foot eight inches; but what he lacked in height he made up in build and that had helped them out of the occasional tight spot during climbs. They made an unbeatable pair in a crowded bar; Eric, with his clear field of vision, would navigate while David applied his shoulders to clear the way.

They had graduated about the same time. While David had gone on to complete his professional qualification, Eric had been offered an opportunity by the University to do a research degree. After completing his PhD, he had been offered a lectureship. They had kept in touch and had continued to climb together when opportunity allowed.

"What do you think about tomorrow?" David went on, changing the subject.

"I haven't seen a weather forecast," said Eric, "but the temperature seems to be dropping. It got decidedly nippy once the sun disappeared and it looks as though we are in for a cold night."

"Well," said David cautiously, "I think rock climbing is likely to be out tomorrow - and that is not just because you probably never ever, ever, ever wish to see another rock face in your life! I should have realised Gimmer was going to be icy."

Eric responded that he was not in a rush to get back on the rock but that he would like to have a go on an easy route before he left if the weather got warmer, just so that he could see that he was not spooked by the fall.

"I'm a bit fed up with flogging up Rossett Gill every morning just to find that the snow on Great End is out of condition. How about trying the Band instead?" David suggested.

Great End is the somewhat inauspicious name for the prominent mountain forming the northern end of a linked group of which Scafell Pike is the highest. Its attraction to winter climbers is the north facing crags rising above Sprinkling Tarn which provide some of the best snow and ice climbing in the Lake District on the rare occasions when they are in condition. In the last two days they had twice struggled over with all their climbing gear only to find the snow too soft for climbing.

Unlike Rossett Gill, which is essentially a stream bed, the Band is a ridge jutting out from the end of the Langdale Valley which provides alternative access to the hills. It divides Mickleden, which gives access to Rossett Gill, from Oxendale, which gives access to Hell Gill and Crinkle Crags. The Band itself gives direct access to Bowfell which at just under 3,000 feet dominates the end of Langdale.

"If snow conditions are any good," he continued, "we could investigate North Gully tucked in behind the north end of Bowfell Buttress. The interesting pitch is near the bottom. On the other hand, if it is like today, we might try Bowfell Buttress. It's another classic Langdale rock route. If I remember correctly, it is better protected than Gimmer Crack."

I think it's graded 'difficult', although it would probably be harder in these conditions. That might give you a suitable rock route with which to re-establish your confidence."

"Hmm," said Eric non-committally.

"Do you want another drink?" asked David.

"Tempting, but I think we should probably go and sort out some supper. Didn't you say that you have a rescue team practice later this evening?" asked Eric. David acknowledged that he did.

"Well, that means I shall be on my own here for a while this evening, so I think we should go and eat and then I can get back here while there is still some prospect of securing a seat. This place is going to be bursting at the seams later this evening with people getting away for the New Year break." The bar was already busier than it had been when they had arrived.

They put on their jackets and made their way out of the bar. It was dark and the contrast with the warmth of the bar was marked. They walked briskly back to the camp site not far from the hotel. The camp site was still fairly empty but would be likely to fill up tonight for the New Year weekend. They were sharing Eric's two man tent. He had just bought it in a sale and was inordinately proud of it. Indeed, the advertising literature, extracts of which Eric had read out in the car, made extravagant claims about water proofing qualities in torrential rain, endurance in hurricane force winds, resistance to ultra violet rays, a lightness which made it ideal for back-packing and a simplicity and elegance of design which would allow a child of six to erect it in five minutes in the dark. They had in fact struggled with it for a good ten minutes in the daylight and to David the end result very much resembled a large red slug. The tent also claimed to be spacious and the literature talked grandly about a 'vestibule' for storage. In fact, like most tents, the only way in was to crawl on hands and knees and, although it was said to be capable of taking two people comfortably, that was only so long as they did not move.

Eric unzipped the front, crawled in and switched on his torch. Another torch flashing nearby showed where two others were putting up a tent. As far as David could make out it seemed to be the double of theirs.

"Snap," he said cheerfully.

"Yes, perhaps we could encourage them to breed," responded a girl's voice.

David grinned and crawled in after Eric. Eric lit a gas lamp and for the next hour they were busy concocting and consuming a culinary delight involving soup, followed by corned beef and baked bean hash with reconstituted mashed potatoes.

Elterwater Mountain Rescue Team advanced base, Friday, 7pm

Just before 7pm David walked a half mile down the Langdale valley from the camp site to the New Dungeon Ghyll Hotel. The so-called 'New Hotel' - it has actually been a hotel since the middle of the 19th century - lacks the age and character of the ODG. Nonetheless, the hotel bar and the bar in the converted barn are the first licensed establishments encountered by tourists at this end of the valley and are consequently popular. They were still fairly quiet, however, at this time of the evening.

Tucked behind the hotel is a large hut. This is the advanced base for the Elterwater Mountain Rescue Team. The name of the team reflected the domicile of most of the original members when it had been formed some 35 years previously. Today most of the members live in Ambleside or further afield and there has been talk from time to time of a name change but nothing has come of it.

Although the team headquarters are still located in a converted barn in Elterwater, it is from the advanced base that most of the rescues in this part of the Lake District are co-ordinated and controlled. The hut is well used. The team are called out around eighty times a year. Some of the call outs are straightforward and involve helping someone off the hill with little more than a sprained ankle. Others are more serious and involve finding, treating and stretchering-off heart attack victims, hypothermic walkers and injured, and occasionally dead, climbers. Very few rescues call for technical mastery on rock or ice, although some of the team members have this; and it is rare that anyone has to be lowered down a cliff on a stretcher, although the team have to be ready should this be called for. The exception is sheep who seem to get themselves into the most impossible positions from which only a harness and a long rope can rescue them, although they show little in the way of gratitude. With most serious rock climbing accidents, the unfortunate victim is generally to be found conveniently but sadly at the bottom of the cliff. The call outs that impose the greatest strain on team resources are the searches for people reported missing in the hills. They sometimes last several days and can cover large areas of the central Lake District and involve a number of teams. In quite a large number of rescues, the team work closely with the rescue helicopter which comes across from RAF Bulmer on the Northumberland coast. The activity going on in the hut this Friday evening was not, however, the result of a rescue but of a training session.

David had been a member of the team for some four years. He had seen a presentation by members of the team one evening about two years after he had started working in the Lake District. He had assumed he had insufficient experience to be of much use in a rescue team but after talking to team members it had been suggested that, if he was interested and had the time, he should give it a try. He had joined as a probationer for a year and after that had become a fully-fledged member of the team. He quickly found that, while all round competence in the mountains is important, so too is fitness and a willingness to devote the time. Living in Windermere was a bit of a disadvantage in the sense that some of the rescues are over by the time he could get to the end of the Langdale Valley, particularly in the height of the summer with all the traffic struggling up the A591. Nonetheless, he felt that he was able to make a worthwhile contribution and he had made some good friends.

The two team Land Rovers were parked near the hut and David could hear laughter. A number of team members were already standing round the table in the hut talking when he went in. Greg, one of the longer serving team members, was recounting the tale of a walker who had recently been caught out by bad weather when crossing from Borrowdale to Wasdale. He had taken shelter by climbing into the stretcher box at the top of Styhead Pass between Great Gable and Scafell Pike.

"That seems like a good idea," said Tom, a team member who had recently completed his probationary year.

"Well, it would have been," said Greg, "except that, when the daft bugger lowered the lid after climbing in, the latch fell into place and he couldn't lift it again."

"What happened?" asked Chris, a new team member, after the laughter had died down.

"He was stuck there for two days. He tried shouting but he couldn't tell when there was anyone near by. Eventually, it seems that two pass-ing walkers came over to have a look at the stretcher box as a matter of curiosity. You can imagine their shock when they opened the lid and found this guy already laid out on the stretcher."

"Was he all right?" asked Chris.

"I think so," responded Greg. "I was talking to someone from the Wasdale team who were called out to help. He was suffering from hypothermia but after being warmed up and given something to eat and drink he was able to walk down."

Greg Meecham was one of the more outgoing and opinionated mem-bers of the team and, at forty nine, one of the oldest. He worked behind the bar at a popular Ambleside hotel. He told a good story, was a bit of a gossip and also tried to give the impression of being a bit of a lad. Unless a person was on the receiving end of one his stories, the combi-nation made him good company with a fund of anecdotes about aspiring hard drinkers and local loose living. His job was not good for his figure; too much time spent on the wrong side of the bar. In the last two years he had started to put on weight around the middle and his pace uphill was beginning to suffer.

While on the theme of stretcher boxes, Joe Henton, the team leader, recounted the occasion when he had been climbing a route on Dow Crag above Coniston. A climber further along the cliff had been experiencing some difficulty while leading a route above the stretcher box at the foot of the crag. Anticipating a fall, another climber who had been eating his sandwiches at the foot of the crag had obligingly, and with considerable presence of mind, held open the lid of the box. In the event that the leader 'bottomed out', he would drop tidily into the stretcher box - to everyone's convenience. There was a communal holding of breath, the leader had duly fallen off but, to a mixture of relief and disappointment on the part of those watching, his second had held him before he landed on the stretcher.

Joe had been team leader for about four years. He was thirty five years of age, of medium height and slight of build which was surprising con-sidering the routes on both rock and snow and ice to his credit. He had become hooked on climbing as a teenager and by his mid twenties he had been amongst those in the forefront of the British climbing world. Like many people in that position he had been exposed to his share of tragedy.

He had been taught early in his climbing career that the sport can be unforgiving of carelessness. A school friend had been killed when an abseil rope slipped off the rock around which it had been looped. Joe had been one of those who had helped to carry the broken body down to the ambulance. The incident made him almost obsessive about safety.

But climbing can sometimes exact payment even from the safest of practitioners. It is possible to guard against objective hazards up to a point but beyond that point there is an element of chance. Chance paid a call in the middle of a route on one of the big Alpine north walls. His climbing partner was seriously injured by a stone fall. It was clear that she needed urgent medical attention if she was to survive. With no help at hand and the weather deteriorating, Joe had had to try and lower her off the face by himself. A sustained effort over fifteen hours had taxed him to the limit and he remembered being surprised at how aggrieved he had felt with his partner when, notwithstanding this effort, she had died before he could get her down.

Joe had given up serious climbing at that point. He had settled in the Lake District, had married a local school teacher and had taken over the management of a climbing and outdoor shop in Ambleside.

He had become involved with the Elterwater Mountain Rescue Team and sometime later had been asked to take over as team leader. Joe had been hesitant about doing so. Climbing had taught him self-reliance and had generated self-confidence. It had not, however, invested him with organisational skills, nor with leadership qualities. Joe was aware that it was these attributes rather climbing ability which were required of a team leader. He was unlucky that these attributes had been tested shortly after he had reluctantly taken up the position. Two separate groups of walkers, one a school party and the other a group of army cadets, had been reported missing at the same time, having both set off from Langdale one very wet and windy Easter. Joe had found himself having to organise and co-ordinate the efforts of four Lakeland rescue teams and a helicopter with very little assistance. Although the cadets had been found fairly quickly, the school party had not been found for three days because the teams were searching in the wrong area. By the time they were found, three of the children and one of the teachers had died. Joe could not help feeling that someone more experienced than himself would have organised the search differently and would have made the difference between life and death.

The outcome of the search had badly shaken his confidence and he had gone through a difficult couple of months when he had seriously considered resigning. Subsequent rescues, however, had been more straightforward and he gradually grew into the position. He remained, however, an essentially modest and self-effacing person. He could never quite get used to the level of assertiveness that was called for on occasion and there was a tendency in the early part of his tenure towards a participative approach to decision-making. While this fostered initiative and encouraged an exchange of views, it promoted differences of opinion and resulted at times in lengthy and indeterminate decision-making. As time passed, he became more confident in his judgement and more decisive about the response; but even now after four years in the post, there remained a collegiate element to decision-making in the Elterwater team. Joe was, nonetheless, now regarded in mountain rescue circles as a capable and experienced leader. His own personal regret about his position was having to stay at Control during a rescue rather than being out on the hill.

One area of the work that Joe had never come to terms with was public relations. He hated the publicity that attended a rescue, avoided the press if he possibly could and was curt and uncommunicative when cornered. He was not especially articulate and was uncomfortable when speaking in public. Yet there was considerable public interest in the work of the team and the team, for its part, relied heavily on public subscription. To get round the difficulty one of the more senior members of the team had eventually been appointed as spokesperson and had spent sometime smoothing ruffled media feathers.

Ironically, Joe found that it was his job as manager of a climbing shop rather than his skill as a climber which was of most benefit to the team. His job meant that the team had access to advice about the latest equipment and clothing and a source of supply on attractive terms. Tonight's exercise was a reflection of that.

Paul Johnstone, responsible for team training, spread out a large-scale map of the Langdale Valley on the table and he and Joe began the briefing for the evening's exercise. Paul was older than Joe and had been a team member for longer. Like quite a few members, he had joined the team because he thought it was about time he put something back into mountaineering, having got so much out of it over the years. His passion was technology, a passion which he never missed an opportunity to communicate to team members. Tonight was no exception.

"OK," said Paul with missionary zeal, "the purpose of the exercise is to give new team members the opportunity to familiarise themselves with the GPS units. The same goes for some of the longer serving members of the team," he added as an afterthought looking across the table at Martin and Greg.

A particularly well-attended sponsored walk organised by the team supporters' group some five years previously had enabled the team to buy enough GPS units for use by all members. Joe had been able to arrange very attractive terms. The units were about the size of portable phones. Some members, however, had been slow to take to them, dismissing them as one of Paul's technological 'toys' and preferring to continue to rely on map and compass. Paul had made it clear that the GPS unit and the map and compass were intended to complement each other but, even so, the units had remained tucked away in rucksack pockets. There had been a similar reaction when 'bleepers' had first been made available to team members to speed up call out times.

Most team members, nonetheless, acknowledged that the technology had its advantages. A number of call outs were now being triggered by the injured party phoning the police and giving a reliable location with their mobile phone in one hand and a GPS unit in the other. This meant that the team could get to casualties very much quicker than might otherwise be the case, thus reducing the risk of hypothermia. There was, however, a down side to the increasing use of technology. Both Joe and Paul reckoned that there had been several cases in the last three years where parties who had got into difficulties had simply given their position and sat back and waited to be rescued rather than attempting to help themselves. Almost certainly there had been several instances in which, in the absence of a mobile phone, a party could have extricated themselves from their difficulties and got off the hill.

"I'm going to take you through the way to use the GPS to determine your position," said Paul. "It is quite straightforward. The unit has other functions as well," he continued, "in particular, you can pre-programme a route and then use the unit to navigate from one point on the route to another; and you can reverse a route. But for rescue team purposes, you simply need to be able to use it to fix your position. The advantage is that the search controller can get an accurate fix on team positions at any point during a rescue without team members having to struggle with a map, compass and torch at night time in the wind and rain. Furthermore, during a sweep search with the team spread out in an extended line across a mountain, it is easier to be confident about plotting the terrain which has been swept."

Paul picked up one of the units. "This is a GPS receiver. GPS stands for the Global Positioning System (GPS). It was developed by the United States for military purposes. It has since been released more widely and navigation in the mountains is only one of the purposes for which it is now used. The system uses satellites to fix your position. If for any reason the unit cannot link up to at least three satellites, it will not work. You could, for example have difficulty in a building, such as this hut, a forest or a gully; it operates best in an open area. It will tell you if it is unable to pick up enough satellites. Assuming a good satellite link, the unit can tell you where you are at any point in time and in any weather by way of a ten figure grid reference. As some of you have difficulty finding your way home from the pub in the evenings, the benefits are obvious."

This sally provoked the expected chorus of groans.

"OK," continued Paul, "you can see that accurate information about your position can be helpful not only for you as a rescue team member but also for the person controlling the rescue. I know you can provide this information from an examination of the map and the surrounding terrain but the receiver offers a simpler way of doing this and it will make life a lot easier at night time. The unit, incidentally, has a built in light".

"A ten figure grid reference seems unnecessarily precise," observed Tom.

Tom had recently completed his probationary year with the team. He was 23, newly qualified as an accountant and an assistant with a firm in Kendal. He was bright, earnest, well-meaning and undeniably competent on the hills. Like Paul, he had something of an addiction to gadgetry. Unfortunately, he was plagued by shyness, an affliction that sometimes made him sound abrupt when he didn't intend to be. His university education set him apart from some of the team and he found it difficult to be 'one of the lads'. He had a tendency to pose awkward, if perceptive, questions and he quite often had an answer for questions posed by others. His problem, as Greg had aptly put it, was that he sometimes allowed his brains to go to his head. As a result, he was the butt of quite a lot of humour in the team. His question to Paul was typical but, in this case, very much to the point.

"Yes, it is," said Paul. "We don't need to know which particular blade of grass you are standing on so we don't use a ten figure reference in practice; six figures is ample for our purposes. That provides a fix within a 100 square metres; so you can round the last two numbers on each axis up or down as appropriate."

"Right," he continued, "would everyone pick up a receiver and switch on." At this point, there was some embarrassment while the more technically challenged team members struggled to switch on the power.

"I want to see if you can provide a grid reference for this hut," said Paul. "Unfortunately, the unit won't work in the hut so we will need to go outside." People reached for their jackets and made their way outside. It was a clear night but the moon had yet to appear.

"All right, the display panel on your unit should show that it is locating satellites," said Paul.

"I can't see a damn thing on mine," complained Martin.

"It would probably help if you switched on the back light for the unit," said Joe, looking over his shoulder.

"My machine is duff," observed Greg after a few moments, "it's not registering anything."

"No, it's not duff," said Joe, "if the receiver has not been in use for a while, it takes a few minutes to get organised. After that, it just takes seconds to fix your location."

"Once the unit has acquired enough satellites it will tell you that it is ready to navigate and will state to what level of accuracy it is operating. Mine shows six metres," continued Paul. He then went on to demonstrate how to turn up the menu page and to select the 'mark' instruction to reveal the current location.

"295066," said Tom reading off the grid reference from his unit.

"Good," said Paul, "spot on. Does anyone else have a reading yet?"

"Teacher's pet," muttered Greg who was still not quite sure what his unit was supposed to be doing.

Eventually, all the units were coaxed into displaying the required position on their screens and the team members trooped back into the hut.

"Right," said Paul, "I'm going to divide you into pairs, each pair to take a radio. Each pair will be given a short triangular course to follow back to the starting point. Control, that's me and Joe, will call you from time to time and ask you to report in your position using a six figure grid reference. I want one of you in each pair to use the map and compass to give the answer and the other to use the GPS; the first to find the answer should call in. This *should* demonstrate the convenience of the GPS. You can take it in turns to use the GPS. This is not a competition, I just want you to feel comfortable with this equipment."

Paul then divided the eight team members present into pairs, gave them details of their short course and allocated them radio call signs. David was paired off with Tania, a lecturer at the physical education college in Ambleside. Although he admired her, he had always found her a bit daunting. She was an attractive and very fit young woman who was not shy of speaking her mind. He had known her through the team for about a year and a half.

Joe drove two of the pairs, including Tania and David, in one of the Land Rovers up to their starting point near Stool End Farm. Paul took the other two pairs in the other Land Rover to their starting point down the Mickleden valley.

Tania and David switched on their head torches and made their way along beside Oxendale Beck. They exchanged information about the Christmas break and their plans for New Year's Eve. She was going to a party organised by some of the staff from the college. He and Eric were planning to spend the evening in the Hikers' Bar at the ODG.

On returning to the base, Paul switched on the base radio and they heard him calling up the first pair: "Langdale Martin, Langdale Martin, this is Control. Do you read me? Over."

The Elterwater team used 'Langdale' as a call sign, simply because phonetically two syllables are easier to cope with on the radio than four. It was also convention to use the name of a member of each group as the call sign rather than a numeral; it was easier this way for Control to remember who was supposed to be where. In this case, Martin and Greg, two of the longer serving team members, had been paired off.

"Control, this is Langdale Martin, reading you strength 5. Over," responded Martin from somewhere near Stool End Farm.

"Langdale Martin, what is your position? Over."

There was a long pause, then: "Position is GR 278056. Over."

"Roger that," said Paul. "Any problems with the GPS? Over."

"I provided the grid reference from the map," responded Martin with a note of triumph in his voice. "Greg is still trying to find the menu on the GPS. What a loser! Over."

Paul groaned. "Try the page button above the power button on the right hand side of the unit," he said, "Out."

The radio was in fairly constant use over the next hour and a half. After a slow start in some cases, and notably from the longer serving members of the team, clear progress was evident. Tania and David managed not to embarrass themselves and by the end of the exercise all the pairs were finding it quicker to report their positions via the GPS.

While most the team adjourned for a quick drink in the bar of the New Hotel, David made his excuses and walked back to join Eric in the Hikers' bar at the ODG.

Langdale Valley, Friday, 7.30pm

Eric, meanwhile, had washed up the supper things after David's departure and then zipped up the tent preparatory to returning to the ODG. As he did so, the couple appeared from the neighbouring tent and they exchanged greetings.

"Are you going across to the bar?" asked Eric.

"Yes, we are," said the girl's voice. "What is it like?"

"Crowded by now, I imagine," said Eric, "but it's got atmosphere."

They walked across together. Jennifer and Stuart, it emerged, were students from Sheffield University in their final year. Jennifer was studying geography, Stuart economics. They were hoping to spend three days in Langdale before moving across to Patterdale to join some friends.

The bar was, indeed, crowded and there were no seats but they were able to find space near the darts board. Eric bought drinks and the three of them were soon reminiscing. Jennifer Halliwell was of medium height, slim with short, startling auburn hair and a ready smile. She would not have been called beautiful, but she had a face of character and held herself well. Stuart Morris was taller with a heavier build, brown hair with a prominent wave through it and a clean shaven face adorned with a pair of rimless spectacles. This was their first visit to the Lake District and the conversation initially focused on what they might do in the morning. Stuart said that they would like to try Scafell Pike as they had not climbed it before but it looked quite a long way on the map. Eric agreed it was worth a visit, particularly in winter conditions, but confirmed that it would be at least a six hour round trip from Langdale, more in winter conditions. If the weather was a bit doubtful, they might think of trying something closer to home like the circuit of the Langdale Pikes or Bowfell and Crinkle Crags. Eric added that he and David were thinking of having a look at Bowfell in the morning.

The conversation moved on to a discussion of other mountain areas. Jennifer and Stuart's normal stamping ground was the Peak District which was easily accessible from Sheffield with occasional trips to North Wales. Eric, who had cut his teeth climbing in North Wales, was soon deeply engrossed in a discussion about the respective merits of the Llanberis Pass and the Ogwyn Valley. From comparing different climbing areas, they moved on to comparing their respective universities and then their respective subjects. Stuart observed to Jennifer that geography seemed to him to be a subject without an object. Eric came to her aid with a story about an economics student who went into an exam and found the paper was exactly the same as one for the previous year. When he queried this with the invigilator he was told that with economics the paper was always the same; only the answers were different! Jennifer seemed grateful for the support. No one could think of anything clever to say about law as a subject.

More people continued to crowd into the already crowded bar and the volume of noise rose to the point where conversation became difficult. Someone struck up with a guitar and someone else joined in with an accordion. For the next two hours a somewhat unstructured and increasingly noisy sing-song developed. It was during this time that David arrived back. It took him several minutes to locate Eric in the crush and he introduced him to Jennifer and Stuart. They did not stay long after that. Eric and David were hoping to make an early start so they decided to leave at about 11pm and Jennifer and Stuart, who were tired after their drive, walked back to the camp site with them.

The sky was crystal clear and there was a bright moon. It was very cold and the ice crunched under their feet as they walked. The camp site had filled up considerably while they had been in the bar. A couple of torches showed where a group were struggling to put up a large family sized tent by the stream which ran through the site. Jennifer and Stuart said good night and crawled into their tent. Eric unzipped his tent and lit the gas lamp while David collected some water from the tap. Then they got the primus going and made themselves a cup of coffee before climbing into their sleeping bags.

In the next tent, Jennifer and Stuart were in their sleeping bags. They had got to know each other through the university mountaineering club. They had gone away for club weekends as part of a group but this was the first time they had been away on their own and this was the first time they had shared a tent.

Stuart had not really noticed Jennifer when he first joined the club although he had remarked on her auburn hair. She was also a new member but he had been more concerned about being accepted by existing members of the club. He had found the transition from school, where he had been a popular senior boy with his own group of friends, to university, where he was unknown, more difficult than he had expected. He had joined the mountaineering club because he had done quite a lot of hill walking and thought he would fit in and he was anxious that the others should know he was not a novice. However, he had found it difficult to find the right balance between, on the one hand, adding a casual and appropriate remark to a conversation which showed he knew what he was talking about and, on the other, saying too much and appearing boastful.

It was Jennifer who helped him to realise that, at the end of the day, acceptance in the club depended more on personality than experience. She was less experienced than he was but it was not something that troubled her. Indeed, she was interested to hear what people had done and where they had been. She was relaxed and a good listener.

Stuart had monopolised her one evening in the bar at a club weekend meet. She had listened politely and with apparent interest to his monologue about what he had done. At the end, she had thought for a moment and then asked whether he really enjoyed mountaineering or whether he did it under some sort of compulsion to collect mountains which he ticked off in a big book. Stuart had been a bit taken aback with the directness of the observation.

He was conscious he might have made a poor impression with her and worried that others in the club felt the same way. After that, he resolved to spend less time talking about his own experience and more on listening. As is so often the case with university clubs, the throughput of students each year raised him quite quickly from the status of new member to one of the crowd. He got to know people and, amongst them, he got to know Jennifer, although he had not gone out of his way to be in her company. Inevitably, they found themselves together on occasions. In particular, they had spent the day together on Goatfell on the Isle of Arran during the club's Easter meet. The other members that day were either attempting the Arran ridge, rock climbing on the cliffs at the head of Glen Rosa or simply touring the island. Jennifer had said that she had never been up Goatfell and would like to go and Stuart, who had not been up either, had agreed to accompany her.

It was one of those long remembered days which seem all too few in the hills when the sun shone in a clear sky and there was not a breath of wind. The view over the Firth of Clyde and the Argyle hills from the summit was unsurpassed. They lay in the heather and soaked up the sun, talking lazily and completely at ease. On the way down, they saw some deer and tried half-heartedly and unsuccessfully to stalk them, hardly surprising with all the noise Stuart made when he stepped up to his waste in a hidden pool. It was a glorious day.

After that, Stewart began to make a point of seeking her out and talking with her at club meets. The weekend in the Lake District, however, had come about almost by accident. A group of them had been discussing the New Year club meet in Patterdale and when discussing transport arrangements, he had said he was thinking about coming up for the New Year weekend itself. Jennifer said that she liked that idea. No one else had been able to get away until after New Year so the two of them had sat down and planned the weekend together.

It had started well. He had called to collect her at her home in Sheffield and Jennifer had put together a quick meal. Then they had joined the New Year traffic wending its way north up the motorway. The trouble had started when Stuart had lost patience with some of the slow moving holiday traffic. He drove very close up behind cars dawdling along in the fast lane trying to pressure them into moving over, generally successfully. On one occasion, however, the car in front had braked and Stuart had had to swerve sharply to avoid hitting it. Jennifer, who had been sitting tight-lipped in the passenger seat, could restrain herself no longer.

"You stupid shit," she exploded.

"Yes, that was bloody dangerous," observed Stuart eventually overtaking the car in question on the inside and giving the driver the finger as he passed. "Asshole," he shouted. "The bastard braked on purpose," he went on in an aggrieved tone. "That could easily have caused an accident."

"No, you idiot," said Jennifer, "it is you I was referring to. You are the menace. I don't remember ever having seen such bad driving. If you intend going on like this, you can drop me at the next town and I'll take the train. Your driving frightens me."

"Please yourself," said Stuart shortly. "Just let me know where you want to get out."

There was silence in the car. Stuart was smarting under the criticism. He prided himself on being a technically competent driver. He liked to drive a car hard but within the limits of control. Usually, his friends at the university found it exciting.

"This is Preston coming up," said Jennifer. "Perhaps you could drop me at the station."

"Oh, don't be silly," said Stuart.

"I'm serious," responded Jennifer. "You really are a rotten driver."

"What do you know about driving?" said Stuart. "I don't suppose you have even passed your test."

"I know a safe driver when I see one. Any fool can drive fast, you simply put your foot on the accelerator. And if it's of any interest to you, I have passed my test."

Stuart was silent for a moment. He didn't want to put Jennifer off at the station. It would ruin the weekend, quite apart from creating logistical problems. Jennifer would have to change trains at Oxenholme and, even then, the branch line only went as far as Windermere. He would have to collect her from there, unless she insisted on taking a bus – and he suspected that would only go as far as Ambleside. He hadn't really appreciated how much he had been looking forward to their two days together. Now, unless he was careful, that was all in ruins.

"Look, I'm sorry," he said after a while. "I don't usually drive like that. I just got up tight with the cars ambling along in the fast lane. How about stopping at the next service station for a coffee? I can unwind a bit. I'll slow down in the meantime if it makes you more comfortable. We are not in any rush."

"OK," said Jennifer after considering the olive branch for a moment and then picking it up. "I think that's a good idea."

They drove in silence for some ten miles until the next service station was announced and then pulled in. Over coffee, Jennifer relented a bit.

"Look, I'm sorry if I was a bit sharp with you, but I really did not feel safe. And then when you swerved after tail-gating that car, I thought we were going to crash."

Stuart always believed that if something had to be done, it should be done well. Although he did not regard himself as a bad driver, he could see, on reflection, that some of the criticism was merited and that an apology would not be out of order.

"Yes, that wasn't sensible of me," he acknowledged. "I'm sorry. I promise to drive like a tourist for the remainder of the journey," he went on with a hint of mischief in his voice.

"In that event, take me to Preston Station this instant!" exclaimed Jennifer with a smile.

Stuart was as good as his word and the rest of the journey passed without incident.

In a way, thought Stuart as he turned over in his sleeping bag, it was a pity that they had met up with the people in the neighbouring tent. He had not had a chance to try and repair the strain on their relationship during the evening. Even so, they were together now and he thought she would welcome a bit of comfort on a night like this and it would show that the argument was behind them.

Stuart snuggled up against Jennifer's sleeping bag and put his arm round her - only to have it pushed firmly away.

"Have I misread the signal?" he asked after a moment.

"Evidently," responded Jennifer.

There was silence for a while. Then Jennifer added: "I wasn't really aware that I had made any signal. You surely cannot have assumed that just because I am prepared to share a tent with you, I am willing to jump into bed with you. We really don't know each other that well. We also spent quite a lot of the journey from Sheffield arguing. I'm not saying we couldn't have a relationship; it's just that you have to give it time."

Stuart was quiet for a moment. Having messed things up, he didn't quite know what to say. Eventually he just said: "Sorry, I seem to have got off on the wrong foot," then he turned over and went to sleep.

Sleep evaded Jennifer for a while. She was not a prude, but nor was she casual in her sexual life. This was partly the result of her upbringing. Her parents had kept a fairly tight rein on her activities during her last two years at school and had continued to try and do so during her first two years at university. She was still living at home, but the demands of university social life were such as to create tensions and she had rebelled against some of the restrictions which her father had attempted to impose. She was unhappy about the hurt which this had caused; but the situation was such that she thought it likely that she would have to look for a flat before long. She was not rushing into this because that would mean finding a job to help pay the rent and she wasn't yet sure how well she would cope with the academic demands of her degree course.

Although she had had tentative relationships with boys during her last two years at school, she had so far avoided any entanglement at university. Those earlier relationships, if they could be called that, had been interesting, exciting, painful, pleasurable but, in the end, devoid of much meaning. They had been part of growing up and she had matured to the extent of wanting to be sure now that her affections were engaged before going to bed with anyone.

She was not ready to commit herself to a relationship with Stuart; nonetheless, she wondered if she had been too harsh with him. Their friendship had taken time to develop and she was not sure if it would go beyond that. When they had first met at a mountaineering club weekend, he had made a poor impression. He had talked a little too loudly and drunk a little too much. He was clearly more experienced than she was in the hills and had not endeared himself by his patronising attitude. On better acquaintance, she had revised her initial impression. She thought he was socially a bit immature and that his talking and drinking reflected this. He was trying too hard to show he was one of the group. On a one to one basis, he seemed more relaxed with a nice sense of the ridiculous. She wasn't sure if he was going out of his way to be with her but they had found themselves in each other's company rather more during recent club meets. She had begun to look forward to his company. He was good looking, fit, intelligent, funny. He had gone out of his way to be helpful in the planning of the weekend and in collecting her from her house. The argument in the car had been partly her fault. She had been a bit of back seat driver, although she thought he had deserved it. Whatever his blessings, they did not include being a careful or courteous driver. The criticism had riled him. Perhaps she could relax a bit with him tomorrow evening. It would be New Year's Eve. She had to admit that, if it was as cold tomorrow night, an arm around her would be a comfort. With that thought she drifted off to sleep.

National Trust camp site, 11pm.

The torches, which Eric and David had seen as they returned with Jennifer and Stuart to their tents, were lighting up a scene of considerable confusion. Two men were struggling with a tent while their partners patiently held the torches. They had come up from London. Peter Stansfield, the unofficial leader of the group, was a middle manager in a large insurance company. In his late twenties, he was well built, with hair already beginning to thin and with the evidence of rather too many business lunches beginning to make itself apparent around his middle. He had an outgoing personality and was a 'social' walker in the sense that he did not take it too seriously but enjoyed the camaraderie of walking weekends. It was his idea to come camping in the Lake District this New Year.

The other man struggling with the tent was Adam Moore. He was younger and quieter than his friend as was evident to the watchers. In the tent pitching stakes, Peter was strong on instruction but weak on achievement. Adam and Peter had met in the Peak District one weekend. They were camping next to each other, had got talking, or at least Peter had, went to the pub together and then went walking together the following day. After that, they had arranged several activity weekends together over the next few years. This was their first visit to Langdale.

Superficially Peter and Adam did not have a lot in common. Peter was extrovert and gregarious. He tended to take the lead in the friendship. Adam was a bit younger, more self reliant and less demonstrative. Physically, he was lean and wiry with a mop of unruly dark hair. He was a civil servant in the Department of Trade and Industry.

Peter and Adam had got to the stage where they now took it in turns to organise an activities weekend. Adam had organised the last one in September and they had both taken their partners. Peter remembered it with some embarrassment. Adam had taken them all down to Harrison's Rocks, a sandstone outcrop near Tunbridge Wells, to try their hand at rock climbing. Peter had a good head for heights and had not thought much of the outcrop when he had first seen it. It was about a third of a mile in length. Nowhere did it exceed 50 feet in height, in some places nearer 30 feet, and the face was split horizontally by ledges that looked as though they should offer plenty of handholds. Not only did it look pretty straightforward but the custom seemed to be to provide a top rope for the person climbing so that there was no danger in the event of a fall. All in all, Peter had been confident he would make a good showing.

Adam, who had been to the outcrop before, had suggested that they start with a reasonably easy climb. He had fixed up the top rope and, as their two companions had hung back, Peter had gone first. To his horror he had found he was unable to get off the ground. He had not appreciated that the face of the outcrop was almost vertical; and that the ledges were all overhung and of sloping sandstone on which it was impossible to get a grip. The climbing required agility, almost gymnastic skills, rather than a head for heights. After ten minutes of scrabbling around he still had both feet on the ground and had had to admit defeat. To his chagrin, their partners, Lucy and Samantha, had both been able to make some progress up the face and Adam had actually made it to the top. Adam had tactfully explained that he had climbed here before and that it was simply a matter of acquiring the rather specialised technique.

They had tried several other climbs on the outcrop over the weekend and Peter had got off the ground eventually. Indeed, he had recovered some of his self respect when he climbed a vertical crack in the face relying on a sequence of jammed hands, elbows, knees and feet. On this occasion it was the girls who had been unable to get off the ground; but Peter's wrists, elbows and knees had been sore for days afterwards where the skin had been sand-papered by the rock.

Peter was determined that there would be no embarrassment for him over the New Year. A weekend camping in the Lake District would give him a chance to demonstrate his leadership skills to the girls and would be something different. Reservations expressed by the others about cold, discomfort and unfamiliar winter conditions were transformed by Peter into challenges to be met. It was all down, he said, to adequate preparation. Such was his enthusiasm that the others had capitulated and entered into the planning of the weekend with a will. A certain amount of new equipment was required and extravagant claims were traded about ice axes purchased at bargain prices, sleeping bags capable of maintaining warmth in coldest Antarctica and boots rigid enough for winter conditions while retaining the flexibility of trainers. Samantha, Adam's partner, had even appeared in a new blue and yellow waterproof jacket with matching waterproof trousers.

"Colour co-ordination," she said, "is very important. It wouldn't do to be seen on the hills in a motley collection of clothing." The material, she assured the others, was guaranteed to keep out the hardest rain while at the same time avoiding the problems of perspiration – not that she was in the habit of perspiring, she added.

Peter had planned the weekend almost like a military expedition. He had decreed that they would leave from his flat off the Edgeware Road no later than 2pm so that they could arrive in Langdale in good time to put up the tent and then adjourn for a bar meal and drink at the Old Dungeon Ghyll Hotel. Like most military planners, Peter was intolerant of departures from his plan and it was with immense frustration that he found himself pacing his living room with no sign of the others at 3.30pm. Had it been possible for steam to come out of his ears, it would have done. He looked out of his living room window for the umpteenth time and willed them to appear. He was a bit surprised when they did. Adam's car turned in to the end of the road and drew up outside.

Peter told himself he would not make an issue of the delay but this determination was rather spoiled when the others also ignored it. Samantha simply said she had been tied up with a patient and had been unable to get away. Lucy disappeared into the bathroom and Adam suggested a cup of tea before they left. Peter, with ill-concealed restraint, reminded them that they had planned to beat the holiday traffic out of London. Adam, who sensed that Peter was annoyed, suggested that they transfer their luggage into Peter's estate car.

This turned out to be easier said than done. In order to ensure their comfort, Peter had borrowed a large family tent from a friend and this occupied a considerable amount of the luggage space. When the collapsible table and chairs, the cooker, gas lights, gas bottle, water carrier, cooking utensils and boxes of food and drink were added to this, there was no room in the back for the personal gear. They had all agreed that they should not stint on the food and drink. Somehow, space had still to be found for two rucksacks, two large bags, four sleeping bags, four pairs of boots and four ice axes. Out came all the luggage and they tried again but with little improvement. Eventually, the matter was resolved by wedging gear on the floor under their feet and on the back seat between Adam and Samantha. They carried their sleeping bags on their laps. It was going to be a cramped and uncomfortable journey.

It was 4.30pm before they eventually got away. Peter almost went ballistic when Samantha announced that they would have to stop at a cash machine as she had not had time to get any money. It was some small consolation to Peter when, as he had forecast, they then got caught in the holiday traffic crawling slowly northwards out of London. He sat tight-lipped in the long line of cars waiting to join the motorway, refusing to join in the chatter and drumming his fingers impatiently on the steering wheel. It was after 6pm before they crossed the M25 and were able to speed up.

Samantha, sensing a bit of an atmosphere in the car, did her best to try and get them all into a holiday mood and with some success. She was two years older than Adam, attractive, tall and slim, with long brown hair. She was an occupational therapist at one of the large London hospitals. They had met when Adam had been visiting a friend in hospital who had lost the use of his legs in a road accident. Adam had helped her in getting his friend on the long haul back towards some use of his limbs and their friendship had grown from that. Although she had little experience of fell walking, she had joined Adam at the last two activity weekends with Peter and Lucy and had very much enjoyed them.

Sam, as she was known, was chatty and outgoing, tactile, with a natural warmth that made her popular with her patients. She applied this warmth now to defusing the tension in the car. She chatted away recounting the challenges of the archery class she had been running that morning for a group of patients with an assortment of missing limbs. She then got them all to describe the most challenging thing each of them had done during the course of that week.

Adam described a meeting he had had to sit in on between a junior Minister and representatives of a local authority seeking government support in a situation of local economic decline. Unfortunately, for whatever reason, the Minister had not read, or had not understood, the brief which Adam had prepared and it was clear that the councillors were expecting the Minister not just to listen but to provide some sort of response. Adam had had to try and extract the Minister from the hole which he had dug for himself and into which he kept falling. The councillors had not been impressed.

Peter, making a conscious effort to overcome his annoyance at their late departure, had talked with growing enthusiasm about a new form of life assurance which would shortly be on the market and which he had been involved in finalising during the course of the week. He recommended them all to sign up at the first opportunity and denied indignantly that the prospect of commission had anything to do with it.

Lucy then recounted highlights from a training course she had been running for young executives during the week. She was a personnel officer - she didn't like the term 'human resources executive' - in the same company as Peter. The executives had played a management game that involved teams building a tower out of Lego bricks. There was a tight time limit for the exercise with marks deducted for towers which were too low or which lacked stability. One team had been penalised for building a sturdy but short tower; another for building a tall but spindly and unstable tower. The third team had sat through the time allocated for the exercise without doing anything and in that way should have avoided any penalty. The team were technically the winners but the course leader had nonetheless penalised them for a lack of initiative. Lucy thought that had been unfair.

Lucy was something of a contrast with Sam. She was reserved rather than outgoing; intense rather than relaxed; small and trim rather than long and willowy; and with features that were too sharp to be thought attractive. Those who did not know her well mistook her quiet temperament for shyness. In fact her quietness belied a considerable degree of self-assurance and determination. Although he would not have been able to articulate this, it was this combination that had attracted Peter. While Peter, rather than Lucy, was the person who would stand out in a crowd, Peter's extrovert nature masked an element of insecurity that needed Lucy's quiet self-assurance for support. In a real sense they complemented each other.

They had met at company social events and she had found Peter fun to be with. They had discovered that they had similar interests in music and theatre. Peter had introduced Lucy to fell walking; but it was something she had taken to without much persuasion. Although small, she was naturally fit and had found in fell walking a welcome release from big city life.

Notwithstanding her reserved nature, Lucy had a good sense of humour and went on to describe some of the strange games invented by management consultants and some of the embarrassing incidents that had happened to participants in these games. This provoked a general discussion about the value of games in management training.

By the time they turned off the M1 to link through to the M6, they were all feeling more relaxed and looking forward to the holiday. Peter, recognising that they were not going to make Langdale in time for a meal, agreed to stop for half an hour at a service station so they could all get a quick bite to eat. It was a quarter to eleven when they eventually pulled into the National Trust camp site. They had been on the road for more than six hours.

Peter immediately set about organising the putting up of the tent. With typical male superiority, Lucy and Samantha, were relegated to the position of torch holders while Peter and Adam got on with the manly task of building the home.

Unfortunately for them, the tent which they were unpacking was wholly unfamiliar to them. Peter had been told by the friend who had loaned it that putting it up was easy. It was a large family tent which they could stand up in with a two room inner tent and a large area under the fly sheet for cooking and eating. This had seemed a good idea bearing in mind the limited daylight at this time of the year. However, putting it up was a different matter. The first thing that struck Peter was that there were a daunting number of poles to be fitted together. It seemed that whatever combination was attempted, and they attempted many, and how ever much they swore at it, and they did so repeatedly, the poles stubbornly refused to create a structure that looked anything like the frame for a tent. Part of the problem was that Peter and Adam, who were accustomed to two-man tents, did not have much idea what it was supposed to look like anyway; although Lucy was fairly sure it was not supposed to look like the very large stick insect which Peter had just created with the poles.

Not only did it not look like the frame for a tent, none of the different combinations of poles seemed to be of the same length and it was clear even to them that at least the four legs of the tent would need to be the same length.

"I think the poles from this tent have been mixed up with poles from another tent," Peter said eventually. "We seem to have too many end bits; and you can see that these poles are thicker than those."

Lucy and Sam had been watching their partners with ill-disguised amusement. Eventually Lucy, who had spotted something which the men had not, could not refrain from observing in a loud whisper to Sam that pitching a tent was clearly a task requiring special skills.

Peter rose immediately to the bait and said huffily that if she, Lucy, thought she could do any better she was welcome to try. Lucy did so. With Sam's help, and with the men relegated to torch holders, she quickly and efficiently assembled in five minutes what clearly was a frame for the tent.

"Well blow me," said Adam. "How did you manage that?"

"Easy," said Lucy, "there are colour codes on the poles if you know where to look. Also the poles for the legs are thicker than the poles for the roof."

"Well, you might have told us rather than letting us flounder around like that," Peter responded shortly.

After that, the tent came together relatively smoothly. Once the tent was up and the gear stowed away, Lucy and Sam unpacked the food for a late meal while Peter lit two gas lamps and got the stove going. The combination of the heat and light, helped by the opening of a bottle of red wine, soon had everyone in a better frame of mind. Adam went to fill up the water container while the girls prepared some soup followed by a spaghetti bolognese. The bolognese was more like a stew than a sauce and the spaghetti was welded together in places but nobody minded that; it was a hot meal and there was plenty of it. By the time that had been cooked and eaten and the dishes washed it was midnight. Peter suggested a night cap to help them to get to sleep and broached a bottle of scotch from their store.

"What are you thinking of for tomorrow?" asked Sam.

"Well, a lot depends on the weather, but if it looks OK I thought we might make our way up the Band to the Three Tarns and round Crinkle Crags," said Peter. He opened an OS map and pointed out the route. "If we manage that without problem, I thought on Sunday we would try the other side of the valley and go round the Langdale Pikes. How does that sound?"

"That sounds good," said Lucy. "Tomorrow's route looks about right for a shortish day - say a three and a half hour round trip. After the long drive, we may not get away much before 11 o'clock."

They talked through their plans a bit more, discussing equipment and what they would take for packed lunch. Then, as they were all tired after the travelling, they got ready for bed.

The Hot Pot, Windermere, 1pm, Tuesday, January 10th

David had compressed all this for Gordon's benefit but he was looking a bit restless as he toyed with his lunch.

"What has all this to do with the rescues?" he eventually asked.

"Ah yes," said David, "the people I have been speaking about were all involved one way or another in the rescues. What I have been trying to do is provide a bit of context for you."

"OK," responded Gordon, "That is helpful. Now provide me with the substance. Can we move to the day of the call out?"

"I was just about to," said David remembering what a bitterly cold morning it had been. He paused again to arrange the events in his mind in chronological order and then continued.

CHAPTER 2

The National Trust camp site, 6.30 am, Saturday morning, 31st December

The National Meteorological Centre, commonly referred to as the 'Met Office', is based at Bracknell. It operates around the clock collating data about air pressure, temperature, rainfall, and wind strength and direction. The observations come from land-based stations, ships, aircraft, balloons and weather satellites. This information is distilled with the aid of computers to provide weather forecasts. These are updated at regular intervals. While it is customary to criticise these forecasts, the 24 hour forecast is now remarkably accurate and the forecast for two to three days ahead is pretty reliable. Beyond that, the variables are such that the same degree of accuracy is not possible; but the Met Office are still able to predict general trends with a reasonable measure of success.

The data coming into the Met Office during Friday night and early Saturday morning showed a mass of cold air pushing down from the Arctic with a deep depression forming over the north of Scotland accompanied by low temperatures and high winds. The forecast as at 6am on Saturday showed this depression moving quickly south to settle on the south of Scotland and the north of England. The forecaster shivered as she looked at the closely packed isobars depicted on the print out for next two days swirling anti-clockwise like a giant Catherine Wheel round that part of the country. "Happy New Year," she murmured.

More detailed forecasts are provided by the Met Office for particular areas of the UK. In the Lake District, the forecasts are supplied to the National Park Weatherline. These forecasts are available to the public at the end of the telephone and are published weekly in the *Westmorland Gazette*.

Eric's alarm went off at 6.30am. David had already been awake for about half an hour, just lying there dozing in the warmth of the sleeping bag. He unzipped the tent door and looked out. In the cold, grey pre-dawn there was little to be seen; sunrise would not be until about 8am. The camp site was quiet and it looked as though there had been a heavy frost but no new snow.

"It looks as though snow conditions should be good this morning which means we could try something on Great End or North Gully on Bowfell," observed David. "I'll see what the weatherman has to say."

He dug out his mobile phone and dialled up Weatherline. The forecast as at 6am reported the present settled period changing for the worse as the day progressed with low temperatures persisting and high winds and snow coming in from the north with accompanying poor visibility. It went on to say that the bad weather would continue through the week-end.

"It doesn't look good," he said. "There's bad weather coming in around the middle of the day - high winds and snow - and it looks as though it's here to stay."

"OK," said Eric, "It's settled at the moment so we have a small window of opportunity - say four hours, to do something. That gives us time to go and investigate North Gully but not much else. If the weather closes in sooner, we can easily retreat down the Band or Rossett Gill."

"Right, let's get off as soon as we can," suggested David.

Eric got the primus going for a cup of coffee but when David reached for the water container it was to find the water was frozen solid. He considered but rejected the idea of holding the polythene container over the stove to melt the water. Accepting the inevitable, he shrugged himself into his clothes and jacket, struggled into his boots, which also seemed to be frozen, and clumped across with the kettle to the water tap only to find this too was frozen. However, the taps in the washroom turned out to be still functioning so he filled the kettle and returned to the tent.

Eric, meantime, had been sorting out some breakfast. Cereal was off as the milk had also frozen. "It's ridiculous," said Eric. "You would expect a camp site like this to have a central heating unit for each tent. Remind me to complain to the warden before we leave." Bread and jam, biscuits, cheese and fruit remained on the menu.

"How about some soup?" suggested David. "I know it's not done in the best circles to serve soup for breakfast, but it really is very cold out there and anything to warm us up would be welcome."

So they opened a packet of dried chicken noodle and sacrificed the water in the kettle to produce a couple of mugs of soup into which they dunked some bread. This perked them up considerably so they followed this with biscuits and cheese and bread and jam and finished off with a banana. While the food was still strewn around the tent, they put together a packed lunch of jam sandwiches, bananas, salted peanuts, and bars of chocolate. David returned to the washroom to refill the kettle so that they could make some coffee in their remaining thermos flask.

Then they dug out the rope, ice axes and crampons from the boot of the car and stuffed their climbing harnesses and a selection of iron-mongery into their sacks. While they were doing this, Jennifer poked her head out of the neighbouring tent.

"Early birds," she commented sleepily.

"Well, it looks as though the weather is not going to last, so we thought we would get off while there is still time to do something," said Eric.

"Where are you off to?" asked Jennifer.

Eric explained what they had decided. "What have you got in mind?" he asked.

"Well, I'm not sure; but, if the weather is turning, we will probably follow you up the Band and have a look at Bowfell."

"OK. Have a nice day! Perhaps see you this evening," said Eric.

"Yes. Bye."

Eric and David strapped their ice axes and crampons to their sacks, David slung the rope over his shoulder and they headed for the Band. Behind them the camp site relapsed into silence.

The Band is one of the 'high roads' of the Lake District. It provides a well-defined route which follows the ridge between Mickleden and Oxendale and takes walkers up some 2,000 feet from Stool End Farm in the valley to a saddle between Bowfell and Crinkle Crags. The saddle is called the Three Tarns. H. H. Symmonds in *Walking in the Lake District* observes that whoever named the place was a pessimist with regard to the number of pools but an optimist in dignifying them as 'tarns'. They are really no more than small ponds of water but usually there are more than three.

They trudged up the Band in silence, plodding steadily upwards, oblivious for the most part of the surroundings, each of them taking refuge from the upward grind in their own thoughts. Towards the top they took a path which branched off to the right across the scree slopes. It was covered in snow today but was identifiable from the old footprints of climbers who had passed that way earlier in the week. This path is called the climbers' traverse and passes below Cambridge Crag to the bottom of Bowfell Buttress and from there it is possible to link through to Rossett Gill. The traverse is straightforward, although at one point the ground below falls away quite steeply towards the valley. A spring emerges from the bottom of Cambridge Crag and provides important refreshment for thirsty climbers in the summer. It was frozen and covered over in snow today. They paused beneath Bowfell Buttress to look at the classic rock route up the centre of the crag first climbed in 1902. They had taken an hour and a half to reach this point. It was now 9.00am.

They decided they deserved a breather before deciding what to do. Eric opened the flask and they shared a cup of coffee while David broke out some chocolate. The buttress faces north east and they had a good view back down the Langdale valley from where they stood. The weather was still settled and there was no wind; but it was cold and the sky was grey and overcast although the tops were still clear.

Bowfell Buttress, itself, looked decidedly icy in places and they quickly ruled out rock climbing as an option. So they picked up their sacks and worked their way along to the far end of the buttress to have a look at North Gully.

National Trust camp site, 9.00am

Back at the camp site, Jennifer snuggled back into her sleeping bag after the exchange with Eric and dozed for a while. Eventually the noise of other people getting up goaded her in action. Stuart was still sleeping beside her. She thought on reflection that she had been a bit hard on him yesterday. She would try and make up for it today; and tonight – well, that was for tonight. It would be good, she thought, to make it a memorable New Year's Eve.

She lent over and shook him with a cheerful: "Wake up sleepy head." Stuart grunted and stirred. Jennifer got into her clothes and made her way across to the washroom. On her way back she paused to take in the view of the surrounding hills. Notwithstanding, Eric's comment about the weather, it was still a clear, if overcast, morning. She returned to find Stuart up and dressed and, while he went for a wash, she got the stove going for breakfast. This comprised a sort of instant porridge made with milk. The milk had remained in Jennifer's rucksack in the tent overnight and had not frozen. The porridge was followed by a bacon and egg sandwich. The latter proved to be a mistake because no matter how carefully they tried to cover the pan, the fat still went everywhere in the confined space. But the activity was companionable. They finished off with coffee and Jennifer used the remains of the hot water in the pan to try and clean up the porridge bowl and the frying pan.

After that they got out the map and picked out the surrounding hills. Once they knew where to look, they could see the path going up the Band and they could identify Bowfell and Crinkle Crags. The tops were still clear.

"What do you think?" asked Stuart. "We could go up the Band to the Three Tarns and then on to Bowfell. Then we could make our way down through the Ore Gap to Angle Tarn and back down Rossett Gill."

"Well, it looks fairly straightforward and Bowfell looks to be worth doing," said Jennifer; "but Eric did mention something about a change in the weather?"

"Yes. Apparently there is bad weather coming in later today. We would need to keep an eye open for that. But if we say two and a half hours to the summit of Bowfell, the weather should hold until we are on our way back down. But if it comes in earlier than we expect, we can always turn round and come back."

"OK, I'll get some lunch together while you sort out our sacks," suggested Jennifer.

Twenty minutes later, they set off for Stool End Farm and the Band. They were about two and a half hours behind Eric and David.

Meanwhile, the noise of people getting up and coming and going had eventually roused Lucy on the other side of the camp site. Unzipping the tent door, she, too, noted that the weather seemed to be settled although it was very cold. She put on the stove for a pot of tea and got dressed and washed. Sam joined her and got out the things for breakfast. Lucy passed cups of tea through to Peter and Adam while Sam cooked bacon and sausages. Breakfast was not to be rushed and the remains were not finally cleared away until 10.30. After that, they packed their gear and checked they all had torches, food and drink, a bivouac bag, water proofs and spare clothing, and an ice axe. Peter went across to the camp site shop to see if he could get a weather forecast and leave a note of where they were going; but no one was around. However, as with many camp sites and hotels in the Lake District, a copy of the 6am forecast from Weatherline was posted on a notice board. It was not promising with a change for the worse coming through later in the day. Peter thought the morning looked settled enough but he acknowledged that the overcast sky could mean anything. Nonetheless, having come all this way, he was determined the group should do something today. He was not unduly worried about the weather because it would be easy enough to turn back if conditions deteriorated. In the absence of any other arrangement, Peter scrawled a quick note setting out their intentions which he left tucked under the windscreen wiper on the car. The note read: "Party of 4. Up the Band. Round Crinkle Crag to Red Tarn. Down beside Pike O'Blisco."

It was around 11.00am when the party eventually left the camp site.

North Gully, 9.30am

Although Bowfell Buttress appears to be a part of Bowfell, it is separated from the hillside by a marked cleft on the south side and by the deeply recessed North Gully on the other side. North Gully was in good condition for winter climbing that Saturday morning. Some of the snow which had fallen during November and December had been protected from much of the recent sun by its north facing outlook; and successive frosts had compacted it so that it now formed a wall of hard packed snow and ice. Although a bit more snow would have been good, the sub-zero temperature last night and the freezing conditions this morning meant that the route was in almost perfect condition for climbing.

The crux of the route lies near the beginning of the gully. After a shallow start, the gully rises steeply to a bulge about 70 feet up before easing off at a point where it tucks in behind the buttress. Eric had insisted that David should have the honour of leading the crux so that he could demonstrate the skills acquired at Glenmore Lodge. He, Eric, had roped himself securely to the cliff at the bottom of the gully in case, he said, the skills proved inadequate for the task and David looked in danger of tobogganing all the way down to the camp site. With these reassuring words, David had worked his way steadily but carefully up the pitch by driving the pick of the two short ice axes he carried into the snow above his head and kicking the front points of his crampons into the slope. He managed to find a small fissure in the wall at the side of the gully for a runner at about 30 feet and he scraped away the top cover of snow and put in a good ice screw at about fifty feet before tackling the bulge. By this time his calf muscles were protesting loudly at the unaccustomed strain of standing on the front points of his crampons for so long. Once the slope eased at about seventy feet, he looked round for a belay and managed to find a convenient crack into which to install some of his larger bits of iron-mongery. He was then able to lean back on the belay and take some of the strain off his legs. After a moment, he cleared a small platform to stand on in the snow - to protests from Eric who found lumps of ice bouncing off his helmet. Then David brought Eric up to join him. By 10.30am both of them were roped to a reassuringly strong belay at the top of the 70 foot pitch.

From there the gully continued at an easier angle but nonetheless required care and Eric led a long pitch to a second belay about two thirds of the way up. David continued on through with the rope but not long after that the gully started to open out and eventually became part of the fellside. David found a large boulder and simply took a turn round it with the rope and brought Eric up.

They had been so engrossed with the route that they had not noticed the weather. The tops were still clear but the wind had risen and was now blowing from the north at about force 5 gusting 6 on the Beaufort Scale.

"This looks like the beginning of the change in the weather," said David. "Let's not bother with the summit of Bowfell and just go straight for the Ore Gap and Angle Tarn. We can then go down by Rossett Gill."

It had been cold in the gully so they already had on their fleeces and wind proof jackets. They took off their harnesses, exchanged their climbing helmets for woollen hats and zipped up their jackets. They then packed the climbing gear into their sacks but kept their crampons on as the snow was quite hard packed at this height. Eric took a compass bearing off the map from the top of the buttress to the beginning of the Ore Gap and they headed off into the wind. After an initial climb, the slope eased off and they skirted the top of Hanging Knotts Crag before picking up a line of small cairns which seemed to be heading in the right direction and they followed this into the Gap. Wainwright, in his pictorial guide to *The Southern Fells,* suggests that the name 'Ore Gap' may reflect the presence of hematite which is evident at this point. Whatever the explanation, it is the name given to the broad gap between the crag known as Hanging Knotts on one side and Esk Pike on the other. They followed the Gap down to join the path from Esk Hause just above Angle Tarn and, after pausing to take off their crampons, made their way down to the tarn to find a sheltered spot for lunch. It was now almost 12.00 o'clock.

CHAPTER 3

The Band, 12.00 noon, Saturday afternoon, 31st December

Stuart and Jennifer made their way in leisurely fashion up the Band pausing from time to time to enjoy the views back down the Langdale valley. Jennifer asked about features they could see and generally encouraged Stuart to compare Langdale with other areas he had been to. They enjoyed a companionable and relaxing progress.

The summit ridge of Bowfell appeared as they neared the junction with the climbers' traverse. Even though the path had disappeared under the snow at about 1,500 feet, the snow had been trampled by booted feet passing this way earlier in the week and there was no doubt about the line and they followed this up to the Three Tarns. The wind had risen and strengthened as they got higher but this was not unusual in mountains and it did not trouble them unduly. The summit of Bowfell was still clear.

From the Three Tarns they turned north and climbed slowly and steeply up towards the summit structure of Bowfell. They were surprised by the force of the wind which hit them as they emerged onto the summit. In view of the force of the wind, they didn't stop there but continued on gradually losing height following the line of cairns in the direction of the Ore Gap. With their heads down, they did not notice the cloud sweeping in from the north until it had blotted out the view and reduced visibility to about five metres.

Then the snow started; not soft, gentle, Christmassy snow but driving, whirling, spinning snow which, with the howling of the wind, made thinking difficult. Stuart was shocked by the suddenness of the change. Inside five minutes good visibility had given way to something approaching a white out, the disorientating condition in which the combination of snow and limited visibility make it impossible to distinguish the ground from the sky. Stuart had not experienced a white out before but he had read about it and could recognise the symptoms. He thought about retracing their steps but decided that losing height as quickly as possible was the priority and the Ore Gap could not be far ahead. With the limited visibility, the cairns were no longer to be seen and the footprints which they had followed had disappeared under the new snow.

Stuart took out his map and compass and with some difficulty in the conditions took a bearing on where he thought the Ore Gap should be. He compensated a little so as to be sure they did not veer too far to the west and end up lost in the head waters of the River Esk. Then with their heads down they struggled on into the wind.

The Three Tarns, 12.30pm

Peter, meanwhile, had arrived at the Three Tarns with his party about half an hour behind Stuart and Jennifer. The group had been going well, although Peter was puffing considerably and realised that he was less fit than he had thought. He vowed to himself he would spend time on the squash court when he got back to London. Lucy had noted the wind getting stronger as they neared the top of the Band, but like Stuart and Jennifer before her, had seen nothing unusual in this. She did, however, give the lead in putting on hat and gloves and getting properly zipped up when they arrived at Three Tarns. Sam took some stick because her woollen hat was not colour co-ordinated with her waterproofs. They then turned south towards Shelter Crag and the Crinkle Crags. The ridge is just over a mile long and, apart from one bad step, is regarded as straightforward. After that, the track heads downhill to Red Tarn and Oxendale. The tops were clear and with the wind behind them and with the shelter provided by Bowfell, Lucy was not worried.

What she had not reckoned on was the suddenness with which the visibility was almost snatched away. One moment they could see clearly, the next cloud had come swirling in from behind them and had blotted out everything. Peter hastily called a halt and took a bearing from the map along the ridge. He had noted from the map that while it was possible to follow the ridge itself, another track followed parallel with the ridge but just to the west. In view of the loss of visibility he suggested that the group stick to the western track so as to avoid anyone straying accidentally into the more precipitous eastern side of the ridge.

Then came the snow which reduced visibility even further. The party stopped to put on their waterproofs. Lucy at that point shouted to Peter that perhaps they should turn back. The Three Tarns were only a short way back and they knew the route down the Band. Conditions seemed likely to get worse. Peter was reluctant to depart from his plan. They had the wind behind them and a straightforward ridge to follow and he felt they should keep on. It would be a shame to have travelled all this way for nothing. They would feel much better this evening if they had been able to complete the walk. However, in view of the limited visibility, he suggested that they keep close together in single file. In view of the difficulty of conducting an argument in these conditions, Lucy did not press her suggestion.

Peter was keeping one eye on his compass but was relying more on the cairns which showed the line of the track. Unfortunately, unknown to him, the track divided beyond Shelter Crag with one branch heading away from the ridge and it was this line of cairns that he inadvertently followed. As the route along the ridge involved a certain amount of up and down, it was a while before anyone realised that there seemed to be too much down in their route. Lucy queried the position but Peter assured her the track was just skirting one of the crags along the way. He thought they were still on course and that they could not expect the track to go in a straight line. Small diversions, he assured her, appeared to be magnified in poor visibility. His view seemed to be borne out by the cairns which disappeared ahead into the swirling snow. Lucy was doubtful but Peter's view seemed to be vindicated when another crag loomed out of the snow and the path diverted down hill to avoid it. However, when it continued on down Lucy realised sickeningly that they had gone wrong. She shouted to Peter and this time he agreed with her.

The question was where were they heading. They held a hurried and shouted consultation. Only Peter had had his compass out and he acknowledged that he had been relying more on the cairns. He thought that in the poor visibility they had probably over corrected after skirting Shelter Crag and strayed through the gap between Shelter Crag and the Crinkles and had been following a line of cairns heading in an easterly direction down into Oxendale. If they just carried on going straight down they would emerge near Hell Gill and could make their way from there to Oxendale and back to Stool End Farm in Langdale. Lucy was feeling disorientated. Her first reaction had been that they had probably strayed in a westerly direction down the Eskdale side. She suggested this to Peter who acknowledged that it was possible but instinctively thought it more likely they were descending into Langdale. Sam suggested retracing their steps to the ridge and then taking a fresh bearing. Peter for once was indecisive; however, having already descended a bit, there was not much enthusiasm for back-tracking. So they continued straight down into the mist with the snow driving in from the side. Lucy had taken her compass out when they had stopped and now she noted that their route downhill seemed to be heading fairly consistently west rather than east. She shouted to everyone to stop and pointed out that they must be heading down into Eskdale. The question of climbing back up to the ridge was raised again but it was felt that they had come down too far now to consider going back. There was still some doubt about Lucy's conclusion. Peter thought they would come out of the cloud before long and that they would be able to settle their position then.

Peter was shocked at how quickly a straightforward day had turned out so badly. He cursed himself for not turning back when Lucy had suggested it. However, whichever side they were on, and his instinct told him they were still heading down into Langdale, losing height was the right thing to do. So they pressed on.

Progress was slow, partly because Peter and Sam tended to be slow movers on steep ground and partly because they were having to be careful with their footing on the snow covered ground. There were plenty of boulders lurking under the snow and a sprained or broken ankle in these conditions might literally prove to be fatal if it meant spending a night in the open. A slip could also be unpleasant and they all had their ice axes ready.

After a while, Peter thought that they must have descended at least a thousand feet but the visibility showed no signs of improving and the snow was driving past as hard as ever. More worryingly, his compass suggested that the slope of the ground had been steering them a bit north of west as they descended so that, if they were going down into Eskdale, they were heading up the valley rather than down it. They had been been following a stream for some of the way in a north westerly direction and this was odd because he thought that should be heading south west if this was Eskdale. If only they could find a sheltered spot where they could look at the map. It was difficult to think straight in this wind and with the snow driving at them from the north.

Angle Tarn, 12.30pm

Angle Tarn had provided Eric and David with shelter from the wind and they had managed to eat their sandwiches and finish the flask of coffee. When they emerged it was to find that visibility was down to about five metres and that the wind had risen. Although they were still reasonably sheltered, David guessed it must be blowing a full gale on the tops of the mountains. As they climbed up towards the top of Rossett Gill, the snow started and by the time they were into the Gill and on their way down it had turned into a blizzard. They stopped to put on waterproof trousers, to pull up hoods and generally to zip up and button up everything that would help to keep out the weather. Then Eric led the way fast down the Gill. It was relief to arrive in Mickleden. The wind and the snow followed them down but they just kept their heads down and made their way along the valley to the Old Dungeon Ghyll.

They arrived at the hotel just before 2pm and made their way round to the Hikers' Bar. It was already crowded with people who had come off the hills and with others who had not ventured out at all. Eric looked to see if Stuart and Jennifer were there but could see no sign of them. Dumping their gear near the entrance, they took off their waterproofs and made for the bar.

"My round, I think," said Eric as he called for two pints.

The warmth and the noise of the bar closed around them. They had timed the morning well and were pleased with their achievement and were now ready to relax.

Hanging Knotts, 1.30pm

It wasn't long before Stuart and Jennifer arrived at the top of Hanging Knotts Crag. The ground dropped away steeply below them into the driving snow. Stuart turned west to try and pick up the entrance to the Ore Gap. Sure enough, almost immediately, the slope beneath them relented and they found themselves at the top of a wide gully. Stuart shouted to Jennifer to have her ice axe ready and then he led carefully downwards. He was alarmed to find as they edged their way down that the snow was hard packed and he shouted at Jennifer to face inwards and kick her toes firmly into the slope as she descended. He glimpsed a rocky outcrop below and made towards it. Jennifer joined him.

"Are you sure this is the Ore Gap?" shouted Jennifer.

"No," he answered, "It's a bit steeper than I thought it would be but it seems to go. Let's try a bit further."

Their problem was that the wind, now a full gale from the north, was blowing the driving snow up the gully into their faces and it was very difficult to make out anything below.

"I suggest we continue to face into the slope and use the ice axe for security," shouted Stuart. "Kick your toes hard into the slope."

As he edged on downwards, it became clear to him that this was not the Ore Gap but some gully on Hanging Knotts Crag. Nonetheless, provided the angle did not get any steeper, he thought they should be all right. The map seemed to suggest a smooth run out at the bottom of the crag to Angle Tarn and it shouldn't be far. He moved slowly so that Jennifer was close to him.

Their undoing was the bendy boots that Jennifer was wearing. They were very comfortable summer walking boots but did not have the steel shank of a winter climbing boot such as Stuart was wearing. The result was that although she attempted to kick her toes into the slope, the boots made little impression against the hard packed snow of the north-facing gully. Stuart realised this too late. He was just beginning to cut a step for her with his axe when her boots slipped and, with a scream, she cannoned into him knocking him off balance. The collision with Stuart slowed her momentum for a moment and she instinctively rolled over on top of her ice axe just as she began her slide down the gully. Try as she might, she couldn't stop herself but the axe acted as some sort of brake on the speed of her slide. She collided heavily and painfully with a boulder at the side of the gully. This, again, reduced her speed although it also broke her left arm below the shoulder and, not surprisingly, had an effect on her use of the ice axe. The speed of her slide started to pick up again just as she crashed into some rocks at a point where the gully made a sharp turn. Fortunately for her the snow had built up against the rocks at the turn and this provided her with a modest cushion. Nonetheless, her crash was severe enough to knock herself out and, in addition to several gashes and severe bruising, she added a broken left leg to her other injuries. The corner, however, stopped her further progress while the snow continued to drive into the gully piling up on top of her.

Stuart was not so lucky. He had fallen sideways as Jennifer cannoned into him and had been unable at that point to use his ice axe. He had bounced off the side wall of the gully on his way down and ended up sliding fast down the gully on his face. He had the presence of mind to try and engage his ice axe but the speed of his slide was such that the axe was torn from his hand as soon as the pick came in contact with the ice. He was travelling fast when he hit the rocks which Jennifer was to follow him into but the impact, although it slowed him, also tumbled him over and he found himself sliding on down the gully upside down and on his back. He tried to turn himself over but this simply brought his head into contact with a boulder and after that he knew nothing. Had he been conscious he would have been reassured to know that his interpretation of the map had not failed him and that he enjoyed a smooth run out on the snow at the bottom towards Angle Tarn. He was stopped from going into the tarn itself by a large boulder which he piled up untidily behind.

Lingcove Beck, 2pm

At around 2pm, the slope which Peter and the others were descending flattened out. At the same time, another beck had come in from the north to join theirs and the two then turned and headed definitely south. Peter called them all into a huddle with their backs to the wind and snow.

"We need to try and work out where we are," he shouted over the noise of the wind. "If we are in Langdale, we could be at the junction of Crinkle Gill and Hell Gill. The difficulty with that is that we should be heading east. In fact, we have been heading west and are now turning south. I think Lucy is right and we have probably come down into Eskdale. This must be Lingcove Beck we have just joined. Can anyone think of any other option?"

Adam looked at the map. "No," he said after a moment, "We have definitely come down a good thousand feet. We can only be in Langdale or Eskdale and the compass suggests we must be in Eskdale. I think we have to work on that basis."

"OK," said Peter, "if that is so, I'm afraid we've got a bloody long walk down the valley to Brotherilkeld Farm which is the nearest shelter. We simply follow the beck all the way. It should be joined by the River Esk coming in from the right after a while."

"Well, the sooner we get on the better," said Adam.

Simply following the beck turned out to be by no means straightforward. Although the map showed a footpath , it had been covered over by the snow and all they could do was blunder along in the deepening snow, trying not to fall over boulders and tussocks or step into boggy ground. Progress remained depressingly slow. The only relief was that, having turned south, the wind and the snow were coming from behind them. All of them by now were, nonetheless, wet and cold and the uncertainty about where they were added to a general sense of anxiety.

Lucy remembered a lecture she and Peter had attended some time ago on mountain first aid. The lecturer had talked about the wind chill factor. Wind speed, he had said, makes a difference to how cold it feels. Suppose, he had continued, a temperature of four degrees Celsius and a wind speed of 25 mph. The effective temperature would then be about - nine degrees Celsius. Lucy thought the temperature at present must be around freezing and the wind speed nearer 40 mph! She didn't know what that meant in terms of effective temperature but it was certainly very cold.

The responsibility for having got the party into this mess was weighing on Peter and he was beginning to feel anxious about the outcome. He should have known better than to rely on instinct rather than the compass. Although not widely experienced, he knew enough about the mountains to recognise the dangers of their position. If only the weather would let up so they could sort out where they were; it was difficult to think clearly in this maelstrom of wind and snow. He started mumbling curses in language he had not used for years.

After what seemed like an hour Lucy was roused from her reverie by a shout from Adam. He had encountered a largish beck coming in from the left and they would have to cross it. The map suggested this might be Swinsty Gill. The crossing was not really a problem but Peter, nonetheless, managed to slip on a rock and fell comprehensively into the water. Notwithstanding his waterproofs, he ended up wet through. There was nothing to be done but press on.

Peter couldn't remember when he had ever felt so wet and cold but, surprisingly, it didn't seem to worry him any more. He began to feel a bit light-headed. He shouted at the weather to do its worst. He felt slightly drunk, which was strange, and realised he was weaving a bit. Then he stumbled and stumbled again.

"Are you OK?" yelled Adam against the noise of the blizzard.

"Of course I am," snapped Peter. In fact all he wanted to do was to sit down and go to sleep. It had crept up on him slowly but he was now feeling very lethargic. It would be wonderful just to lie down and let all his cares float away. He carried on a bit further before stumbling again.

"Think I'll jus resht for a bit," he said promptly sitting down in the snow.

"We can't stop here," said Adam worried by Peter's action. "We need to find a boulder or something for shelter if we are going to rest." Peter just sat there. He felt as though nothing mattered any more. All he wanted to do was lie down.

"Come on," said Adam, "we must move on a bit," and he and Lucy helped Peter to his feet.

They struggled on through the blizzard but after another five minutes Peter sat down again. Adam and Lucy were by now both very worried. Neither knew very much about hypothermia but they knew enough to recognise some of its symptoms and Peter was exhibiting these. Adam looked around but the blizzard still restricted visibility to a few metres.

"I think we should press on a bit further if you feel you can," he shouted. "If we can find some shelter, we can have a good rest." He helped Peter to his feet again only to find him subsiding into the snow after a few steps.

Sam, meantime, had just been standing there without seeming to take in what was going on. She was the least experienced of the party and had found the conditions frightening and the descent exhausting. She was now colder than she had ever been and her mind seemed to be withdrawing into a world of its own. Lucy noticed that she was shivering.

"Are you OK?" said Lucy into her ear.

"I think so," answered Sam, dragging herself back to the awful reality. In fact, the attraction of sitting down with Peter on the ground was almost overwhelming. Lucy took her sack off and rummaged around in it for her flask and some chocolate.

"Here," she said, "have a hot drink." Sam took the cup while Lucy broke up some chocolate and handed it around. Adam, meantime, took out his flask and poured a cup for Peter.

"What do you think?" yelled Adam to Lucy. "Should I just go on ahead a bit and see whether there is any shelter?"

"I don't think you would find us again in this weather," shouted Lucy. "We all go on or we all stop; and I don't think we can stop here." She retrieved the cup from Sam and poured herself a hot drink. Adam had some too and then they packed away the flasks.

"Can you give me hand with Peter?" he asked. She nodded and signalled to Samantha to help. Samantha just stood there.

Together, Adam and Lucy got Peter on his feet again. Adam put Peter's arm over his shoulder and Lucy took the other one. Together, they stumbled slowly along beside the beck. After a while, Peter fell and dragged Lucy down into the snow. She scrambled to her feet again and noticed to her horror that Sam was nowhere to be seen.

"Where's Sam?" she yelled to Adam.

"She must be coming along behind," he said without conviction.

"You stay with Peter, I'll go back for Sam," said Lucy. "Look, is that a rock of some sort over there?" She pointed to what looked like a snow-covered hump of some sort barely visible ahead through the driving snow. "I'll give you a hand to get him over there and see if you can make some sort of shelter."

Together they more or less dragged Peter through the snow to what looked like the ruins of a sheepfold. The wall had fallen down but the far side of the pile of stones gave some limited shelter from the wind and snow.

"I'll see if I can build up the wall a bit," shouted Adam.

"I'll go back and see if I can see Sam," yelled Lucy. With that she took out her compass and noted the bearing as she set off back the way they had come. Fortunately, their footprints from the struggle with Peter were still visible and she backtracked. She found Sam after a few minutes just sitting in the snow.

"Sam," she shouted, "Come on, we've found a bit of shelter up ahead. I'll help you up there and then you can rest."

Sam muttered something which Lucy didn't catch. "Come on, we've found some shelter," she yelled again.

She reached down and tried to help Sam to her feet. Sam angrily shook her off. Lucy felt some relief at the show of spirit in place of the previous lethargy.

"Come on Sam, it's only a little way on. Promise." This time when she reached down, Sam allowed herself to be helped to her feet. Taking Sam's arm round her neck, they struggled forward through the snow. The footprints were still visible so she didn't need her compass. Soon they came to the sheep fold. Lucy lowered Sam down next to Peter and then helped Adam to try and raise the height of the wall. It was hard work because the stones had bedded themselves into the ground over the years. Eventually they managed to raise it to about three feet.

"Let's get them into their survival bags," said Adam. Lucy unclipped Peter's sack and took out his orange polythene survival bag. Lucy took Peter's boots off and together, with a bit of assistance from Peter, they got him into the bag. Lucy then unpacked Sam's survival bag and Sam struggled into that.

"Snuggle up against each other," shouted Lucy. See if you can generate some body warmth between you." With a bit of pushing and shoving they shifted Peter and Sam as close together as they could. Lucy then checked the sacks but all available clothing was already being worn

"What now?" said Lucy to Adam.

"One of us must stay and the other must try and get help," he replied crouching down in the shelter of the low wall. "I'll stay and see if I can improve the shelter. I will then see if I can join Sam in her survival bag. You still seem in pretty good shape. You've got a compass and know how to use it. Here's the map; don't lose it, it's our only one. Keep the river on your right and just keep heading south west until you come to the farm. It's still quite a way so take it easy."

Lucy thought about arguing over who should stay but eventually accepted Adam's suggestion. "OK," she said. "Take care." She gave him a hug, went over to say goodbye to Peter and Sam, picked up her sack and headed off into the snow.

Adam set about trying to improve the shelter. Over the next half an hour, he managed the raise the wall a bit further and packed snow into the gaps. He then collected all the rucksacks and checked the contents. He folded one to raise Peter's head off the ground and provide a sort of pillow and then did the same for Sam. He collected all the food and drink together and tried to get Peter to drink some hot fruit juice. Peter had lapsed into a stupor and Adam had to prop him up while he tried to get him to drink. He ended up spilling most of it. Sam was more responsive and seemed to recover a bit after a drink. Adam fed her some chocolate and then with some difficulty managed to squirm his way into the same survival bag so that they lay there with their arms around each other with Sam slowly benefiting from his body warmth. It was now 3.30pm.

Hanging Knotts Crag, 2.00pm

Jennifer slowly emerged from unconsciousness into a world dominated by the howling wind and driving snow. She came out of a peaceful, drifting greyness into a brutal, noisy, uncomfortable, painful and curiously white reality. For a moment she lay there huddled against the rock in blank incomprehension. Then the full enormity of her position came to her; and when it did so she was gripped with a blind panic. Her first reaction was to call out for Stuart but she might as well have shouted against a cheering football crowd; her voice was simply whirled away in the wind. She had not realised the weather could be so noisy. She knew he must be somewhere below her; and, having fallen further, she recognised that he was probably in a worse condition than herself.

Her immediate concern was that she might fall further. Her position seemed precarious and she had no idea how much further it was to the bottom. Visibility was limited and all she could see was the gully disappearing down into the cloud with steep cliffs on either side. She wondered about trying to work her way down with the aid of her ice axe but, having no idea what was below and realising from the background of pain that she had not escaped uninjured from her fall, she quickly rejected the idea.

It dawned on her, nonetheless, that, unless by some miracle Stuart had escaped unscathed, there was little prospect of help for hours to come. She was on her own and, if she didn't fend for herself, no one else was about to. She remembered she had mentioned to Eric that they might be going up Bowfell; but how long would it be, if ever, before Eric noticed they were missing and alerted the mountain rescue? She thought he would allow them a good margin of time to get down before doing anything. Even then, what prospect was there of anyone finding her in this blizzard? She was aware of the consequences of prolonged exposure to the cold and doubted whether she could survive for long in this cold. She would probably die during the night unless she was rescued. The more she thought about it, the more the panic started to reassert itself.

It took an effort to try and think more positively. At least she was alive - so far. Her first priority had to be survival and for that she needed to secure her own position and to make it as sheltered as possible. On examination, she found that by a curious stroke of good fortune, if such it could be called, she had ended up in a sort of elbow in the gully and that the rock wall of the gully provided a limited shield from the weather. It was the combination of the crook of the elbow and the shield which had stopped her slide down the gully. Although her position was still precarious, she thought that, if she could excavate a bit of snow and ice out of the gully, she could create a better shield and at the same time give herself more room and greater security. The elbow itself was inclined rather than flat but it might be possible to improve on that by cutting out some of the ice. Fortunately, her ice axe had not parted company with her and was still dangling from her arm by its wrist strap.

However, when she attempted to move, she was forcefully reminded that she had not escaped from the fall unscathed. The pain had been there all along in the background but she had not had the courage to investigate. Now she forced herself to do so. Although she had banged her head, gentle probing suggested a bit of a gash and some bruising but no break. The act of probing, however, showed her that there was something wrong with her left arm. There was a numbness around and below the shoulder. Movement of the arm was possible, although painful; but there was a general weakness and she suspected it might be broken. Further examination suggested her ribs and pelvis were OK and so was her back. What she was worried about, and rightly so, was her legs. A little testing made it painfully clear that the crash into the elbow of the gully had broken her left leg below the knee.

Well, it could have been a lot worse, she thought, determined to try and see things positively. She would have to be careful with the leg; but she was not so disabled that she could not help herself. Over the next half an hour, she worked slowly and painfully to clear the snow and ice from the elbow of the gully so as to create a flatter, larger and better protected platform. At times the pain from her leg caused her to cry out and on one occasion the pain was such that she thought she was going to pass out again. At the end of that time, she felt she was now reasonably secure against a further fall, although she would have to continue to be careful. Then she set about making herself as warm and as comfortable as she could. The warmer she could keep herself the more time she would buy for herself and the more time the rescue team would have to find her. She had a spare jersey and survival bag in her rucksack. With some difficulty and not a little pain from her arm she eased off her jacket, shrugged on her additional jersey, put her jacket back on, pulled her woollen hat firmly down over her ears, put up her hood and zipped and buttoned herself up as tightly as she could. Then she struggled into her survival bag, again nearly passing out from the pain when she could not avoid moving her leg. After that, she had exhausted herself. So placing her rucksack so as to provide a cushion against the rock wall, she lent back and closed her eyes while the storm raged on around her.

River Esk, 4 pm

With very mixed feelings Lucy left Adam working to raise the wall of the sheepfold and headed off down what she was almost certain must be the Eskdale valley. She was unhappy to be abandoning Peter and Sam when they were clearly in a bad way. Peter, in particular, seemed to have passed into a world of his own. On the other hand, she was realistic enough to know that unless one of them could get help fast, his prospects of survival were not good. She thought Adam would do a better job than she could of improving the shelter and as she was still feeling reasonably fit, she was not unhappy to be doing something obviously useful.

It was a challenge for her and, while she had no illusions about the seriousness of the situation or of the conditions she faced, she was a determined woman. Well, she would need all her determination now.

It was a help that the wind and the snow were coming from behind; but the snow had been settling for some time now and the increasing depth made walking difficult. She found she had to lift her legs higher with each step than was comfortable and this was very tiring and also made for slow progress.

The compass showed that the beck was continuing to head in a generally south westerly direction. She thought she could not be far from the junction of Lingcove Beck with the River Esk, if indeed this was Eskdale at all. The lingering uncertainty was a continuing source of anxiety. However, to her great relief, after about half an hour of staggering through the snow, she noticed a bridge across the stream and just after that a river joined the stream from the right and the combined flow continued on to the south west. She was now sure of her position and this gave her a bit of a lift so that she pressed on with greater confidence.

However, the light, such as it was, was rapidly going and it wasn't long before she had to slow right down because of the dark. She stopped and rummaged in her sack for her head torch. She then strapped the band of the torch around her woolly hat, angled the lamp so as to give her the best light, put her hood back up and continued on her way. The light from the torch did not amount to much but it was better than nothing. The worrying thing was that she was having to pick her way and this made for even slower going than before.

She crossed a stream coming in to join the river from the left and sometime after came to another. It was just a small stream but the far bank, as she stepped across, deceived her. Her foot disappeared into a hole in the bank and the weight of her body as she came forward on it severely wrenched her ankle. Lucy collapsed with a cry into the snow.

For a moment, everything was too much for her. The combination of the pain, the howling of wind, the driving snow and the impenetrable dark overwhelmed her for a while and she lay there sobbing. She felt more frightened and alone than she had ever been. Any movement of the foot was agonising and she thought she must have broken her ankle. After a while, the pain seemed to ease a little and she tried moving the foot only to be submerged by more spasms of pain. She was aware that a cold compress was sometimes considered effective in calming the swelling associated with a sprain and she wondered about plunging her foot into the stream to cool it down. One thing was clear. Unless she could ease the pain, she would not be walking on the foot for some little while; and if she could not walk, Peter would die and Adam and Sam would be at risk. So would she, she added to herself as an afterthought.

Easing herself forward she gingerly lowered her boot into the water. She gasped as the icy cold water worked its way into her boot and her immediate reaction was to withdraw the foot. "Chicken," she thought lowering it back into the water again. She found she could only bear the cold for a short while before having to remove her foot. She tried this for half a dozen times before deciding she had had enough.

She wasn't sure whether it had helped or not but it was done now; the pain seemed less noticeable but that might simply be because her foot had gone numb. She decided she should give the ankle a bit of a rest and searched with her head torch for anything that might offer shelter from the blizzard. There were no boulders in sight so she picked out a tussock which seemed marginally bigger than the rest and dragged herself to it. Then she got out her survival bag and with some difficulty eased herself into it. She tucked herself in behind the tussock, made a sort of pillow with her rucksack and lay down. There was no risk that she would go to sleep, she didn't feel the least bit sleepy; but she thought that twenty minutes rest might do the foot some good.

Hanging Knotts, 4 pm

Stuart slowly emerged into a world of pain. He could make no sense of it. There was noise and a whiteness everywhere. He had no recollection of where he was, nor how he had come to be here. He was cold. He thought he might be dying; perhaps he was already dead. He tried to move but the pain surged over him like a tidal wave and he relapsed in unconsciousness.

Jennifer meanwhile had managed to rest; indeed, she had managed to doze on and off but had come too with a feeling of suffocation to find the snow piling up on top of her. Every so often she tried to clear it out but it seemed to return as fast as she could remove it; and any movement on her part seemed to be an invitation for pain to reassert itself. The constant ache from her shoulder and her leg was debilitating. After a while she had reached into her sac for her flask and had allowed herself half a cup of coffee, some chocolate and a bit of mint cake. She realised she would have to ration her provisions. It was unlikely she would be found while this weather lasted. She doubted whether anyone would be passing this way until it blew itself out. She would have been upset had she known that while she had been dozing two parties had gone past on the track by Angle Tarn. They had been struggling back from Great End heading for Rossett Gill and Langdale. It would have made no difference if she had known. They could not have seen her in the blizzard and they would not have heard a shout above the noise of the wind. All in all, it was better that she did not know.

She remembered her whistle. She dug around in her sack until she found it. She could not remember the distress call but she thought it was six blasts a minute. If nothing else, she thought Stuart might hear it and know that she was still alive. She soon gave up. The howling of the wind seemed to mock her efforts. She would try again when the wind died down. In the meantime, she huddled up, pulled the top of her survival bag more tightly together to keep in the precious warmth and thought about the warmth and noise of the Hikers' Bar and New Year celebration they had been looking forward to. Presently, she relapsed into a doze.

National Trust camp site, 4.30pm

Eric and David had enjoyed a relaxed afternoon in the Hikers' Bar at the ODG. This had filled up as people came in off the hills or came across from the camp site. With the blizzard setting in, no one was contemplating an afternoon in the hills and there was little to do on the camp site. Eric kept an eye open for Jennifer and Stuart. Eventually, around 4 o'clock they decided to go back to the tent and make a meal. With the heavy snow, there was no point in driving anywhere for a meal and they felt like a change from the bar.

When they got back to the camp site, they noticed that Jennifer and Stuart were not in their tent. David suggested that perhaps they had decided to leave the hills alone today and had gone off into Ambleside or, maybe, Kendal instead. Eric pointed to a car parked near the tent. Stuart had been complaining about being 'rear-ended' in a minor way by a car travelling too close behind him about a week ago. He had shown them the dent on their return from the bar last night. They both went over to have a look. Sure enough there was an evident dent affecting the back bumper and boot. There was nothing to indicate that the car had been moved all day.

They made their way back silently to the tent and lit the gas lamp.

"You're worried aren't you?" said David.

"Yes, although perhaps it's a bit early to be really worried. They could have gone for a walk over to Little Langdale or simply gone down to the bar at the New Dungeon Ghyll. I guess we should leave it a bit longer."

"Why not leave it until 6pm," David suggested. "If they are not back then, I think we should check the Hikers' Bar and the New Dungeon Ghyll. If they are not there, then we should phone the police. I would rather get the rescue team out too soon than too late."

"Yes, so would I," said Eric, then changing the subject: "What culinary delights are you proposing to tempt me with this evening?"

"Well now, I thought we might start with a hint of sun-ripened tomatoes simmered gently to a fine soup, followed by essence of pampas fed beef with flaky potatoes and succulent beans in a rich sauce; and to accompany it a deep red nectar with an aroma of ripened fruit and a suggestion of summer in Tuscany."

"So it's tomato soup, followed by corned beef hash washed down with Italian plonk - again!" said Eric. "Your adventurous spirit does you credit."

"Well you know how fussy you are when I try something new," responded David in an aggrieved tone.

"No, that is not strictly accurate," said Eric. "I only made a fuss because you had burnt the meat to the consistency of tank armour last time you tried something new and dropped the rice on the ground while you were draining it. Then you scooped up the rice and put it on my plate along with bits of grass, some earth and a sprinkling of rabbit droppings."

"There is no pleasing some people," observed David.

By the time they had finished the meal there was still no sign of Jennifer and Stuart. They put the kettle on to boil for coffee and speculated about what might have happened to them. It was an unproductive discussion because they had no idea whether they had stuck to their original intention of going up the Band to Bowfell. Although they talked positively, in the back of their minds was a fear that they had run into difficulties - in which case the longer they delayed in alerting the rescue services, the longer they would be at risk. As it was nearly 6pm, they decided to have a quick look in their tent to see if there was any indication where they might have gone and then they would check the ODG and the bar at the New Hotel.

The tent revealed nothing except that Jennifer and Stuart had more imagination than them as regards menus. Packet curries and pasta dishes were evident. A further check of the car also showed no messages attached to the windscreen or otherwise evident. The Hikers' Bar was still crowded but there was no sign of them. As the snow was still falling and the road had not been cleared, they walked the half mile down to the New Dungeon Ghyll only to find they were not there either.

"So how do we alert the mountain rescue team?" asked Eric.

"We don't," David responded. "We dial 999 and alert the police. They contact the rescue team. But it might be sensible for me to have a quick word with Joe, the team leader, just to put him in the picture."

David had brought his mobile with him and put a call through to Joe. When he answered, David quickly outlined the position. Joe thought for a moment: "It doesn't look good, does it?" he said eventually. "Have you seen the weather forecast?"

"Not since this morning," said David.

"Well it's set in for a couple of days and is supposed to be getting worse before it gets better. I suggest you put a call through to the police and I will start setting things in motion this end. This could be difficult as it's New Year's Eve. We may find ourselves short of team members. You might as well hang on there until we arrive. Did you leave a message in their tent asking them to contact you should they return?"

"Er, no," said David. "I'll go and do that after I've phoned the police."

Eric said he would make the call as he had always wanted to dial 999.

The Hot Pot, Windermere, 2pm, Tuesday, 10th January

Gordon stirred his coffee thoughtfully. "I had not realised you were so intimately involved in this particular rescue," he said. "You realise that you or Eric are likely to have to give evidence at the inquest."

"Yes, that had occurred to me," said David.

"The way in which you have related this to me means that, at the time of the call-out, I know what has happened to the parties on the hill. Of course, the reality is that you and Eric and, more importantly, the rescue team leader – Joe Henton – did not. You were having to make an informed guess about what might have happened and Joe had to commit his resources on that basis."

"That's exactly right," said David. "I thought it made sense to give you the material chronologically. But if you are to understand why Joe and others made particular decisions, you must keep in mind that until we found the casualties, we were not sure there had even been an accident."

"If we continue chronologically through the events of that weekend, the next stage is the rescue itself," said Gordon. "Take me through the call out procedure and what happened once the team was assembled. Try and tell me what it was like for those involved."

David had a clear picture in his mind of Eric, sitting in the New Dungeon Ghyll Hotel, thumbing 999 somewhat nervously on his mobile. He took Gordon through the call out arrangements and went on to relate in detail the events that followed over that weekend.

CHAPTER 4

Call out, 6.30 pm, Saturday evening, 31st December

Emergency services. Which service please"? It had been a quiet evening so far on the switchboard and Sandra had been reading a book. All 999 calls in the Cumbria Constabulary area come to Carleton Hall outside Penrith. Sandra was looking forward to finishing her shift at 8pm and getting away to enjoy New Year's Eve.

"Police," said Eric.

There was a slight pause, then a voice said: "This is the Police. What is your name please?"

Eric gave his name.

"What is your telephone number?"

Eric asked David and then passed on the number of his mobile.

"Where are you phoning from?" asked the voice.

Eric responded that he was phoning from the New Dungeon Ghyll Hotel.

"What is the problem?" asked the voice.

Eric explained that a couple in the tent next to theirs had said that morning they were going up Bowfell and had not returned. He thought something must have happened to them.

"Thank you for the information," said the voice calmly. "Please remain where you are. The police will be on their way shortly and will wish to talk to you further about this. We will contact the mountain rescue service."

The information was passed through to Windermere Police Station and Constable Matthew Harman at Chapel Stile in Langdale was asked to go up to the New Dungeon Ghyll Hotel to speak to Eric Burns and get more details. In the meantime, Sergeant Bill Williams who acted as police co-ordinator on mountain rescues in the southern part of the Lake District, was alerted and set off in a police Land Rover for Langdale.

The arrangement which the police have with the Elterwater team is that the police alert the team leader and the deputy team leader by bleeper. In this case, Joe had already had a quick word with Alex Frost, his deputy, in anticipation of the call. It had been agreed that the team would assemble at the Elterwater base to avoid everyone having to struggle in their cars in the snow to the end of the Langdale valley. Alex immediately headed off to Elterwater to open up the base and to start putting together the gear they would need. Joe responded to the bleeper by phoning the police and Eric's message was relayed to him. Joe said he would be setting up control at the advanced base at the New Dungeon Ghyll and it was arranged that Sergeant Wilson, the police co-ordinator, would meet him there.

Joe then alerted the rest of the team by triggering their individual pagers. A message in the form of a numerical code was passed. The numerical code indicates the assembly point for the team with a different number for each of the more common assembly points. In the case of an unusual assembly point, the pager will indicate that team members should phone a police voice mail box and a recorded message will explain the arrangements. In this case, the code meant that the team should assemble at the Elterwater base.

When his pager went off, Stephen was just finishing his evening meal. He was the National Park ranger covering the Langdale area and had been a team member since taking up his post four years previously. He had seen the forecast that morning thought it likely that the combination of New Year weekend and bad weather would result in a call out and had had an early evening meal and his rucksack and winter gear were all ready. Living in Chapel Stile, he was close to the rescue base so he quickly made himself a large flask of hot, sweet fruit juice, put on his fleece and jacket and his boots and gaiters, collected his sack, ice axe and crampons and then shut up the cottage As it was still snowing hard, he decided to walk the half mile or so to the base.

Greg was not so lucky. When his pager went off, he was just sitting down to his meal. His wife, Marion, had just taken a piping hot lasagna out of the oven and was dishing it out. Greg cursed fluently, partly a reaction to a ruined meal, partly the prospect of going out on a night like this, and partly the thought of missing the New Year party he had planned to attend. He scraped his portion of the meal into a cereal bowl, asked Marion to make up a flask and went to collect his gear. His rucksack was more or less ready but in view of the weather, Greg stuffed another jumper into it along with some chocolate, collected his ice axe and crampons, made himself a thick jam sandwich and put on his boots. He phoned Martin, who lived near by and arranged to pick him up. Marion wedged his flask into the sack and went out to start the car. Greg put his gear in the boot and then climbed into the passenger seat with his bowl of lasagna and a spoon and they set off.

"Oh bugger," he exclaimed after taking his first mouth full, "I forgot to add the Parmesan cheese!"

Andrew was driving into Ambleside when his pager went off. He was just finishing his shift for the day and was feeling tired. Driving a bus in the snow was not the most relaxing of occupations, particularly when he was driving on an unfamiliar route. He had even got lost at one stage on a minor road in the middle of nowhere. He remembered the bemused faces at the bus stop on the other side of the road when he had slid open his window and asked if anyone knew where his bus was supposed to be going. Fortunately, he had acquired a passenger who knew the route and the problem had resolved itself after that. Now he was looking forward to a bath and evening meal. He had planned to spend a quiet New Year's Eve with his wife. She would not be pleased seeing it in on her own. Having checked his bleeper, he drove his bus to the bus station, explained the position to his supervisor, and headed for home. As he passed the fish and chip shop he saw there was hardly any queue and, suspecting a long night ahead, he bought a large portion of haddock and chips. Once home, he picked at the fish and chips while his wife Pam helped him to get his gear together. Then he set off in his car for Elterwater, his fish and chips open beside him, calling in to collect Roger and Heinz on the way.

Heinz was one of the three team dogs and Roger was his owner. The name 'Heinz' reflected the dog's breeding. While it would be defamatory of Heinz to suggest 57 varieties, he was clearly made up of a bit of this and a bit of that and a lot of collie. He was a trained search and rescue dog and very much enjoyed rescues. His only fault was an excess of enthusiasm. He had been known in the excitement of finding a casualty to jump all over the injured person, not a recommended response to a broken leg. And sometimes the first an injured person knew of the arrival of the rescue team was a vigorous face licking. Nonetheless, Heinz had a number of finds to his credit and his somewhat daft good nature made him a favourite with team members. Roger, a teacher at the local comprehensive school, sometimes felt he was better known as Heinz's minder rather than as a team member in his own right. Heinz clambered obediently into the back of the car casting a wistful glance at Andrew's supper.

Shelagh was in the bath. She worked as an instructor at an outdoor pursuits centre near Ambleside and today had been a work day. She had been out with a party doing ice axe practice on Fairfield. They had had to go quite high to find a decent snow slope. She had been aware of the anticipated change in the weather and she had brought the group down to Rydal for a late lunch and had then walked back under Loughrigg in the snow. Shelagh had been a team member for about a year and a half. A friend at the centre had suggested she might be interested in joining the team. Shelagh had expressed reservations about sticking her head into a male preserve but had been assured that there was nothing to fear and so it had turned out. She had found that, with the possible exception of stretcher carrying, she could contribute as much to a rescue as the men. She cursed as her pager went off and reached for a towel. She had been looking forward to a cosy evening and to joining some friends to see in the New Year later. She put on dry clothes, picked up her damp fleece, jacket and windproof trousers, re-packed her rucksack and set off for Elterwater

Paul, the team training officer, was flat on his back with his head under a sink when he heard the pager. He eased himself out and reached for his jacket to check the message. Then he crawled back under the sink. He had been called to deal with a burst pipe. This was a busy time for plumbers and with the pipe work in bits he was in no position to rush off. He would go along as soon as he had finished the job. He had a feeling that the pager heralded an all night job so he would still be in time to help. He picked up the wrench and turned his attention back to the job in hand.

Alex, the deputy team leader, was the first to arrive at the Elterwater base. He painted for a living and ran a studio in Ambleside. He had given up a job in industry to come and live in the Lake District. He had picked up odd jobs for the first couple of years while he tried to make a go of painting. In fact it had taken him five years before he could launch out on his own but he had never regretted it. He had been a team member for about ten years. This was a quiet time of the year and he used it to build up a stock of paintings for the summer. He had been out this morning photographing some of the winter colours for use later. He had planned to attend a ceilidh in Ambleside with his wife and a group of friends to see in the New Year. She would have to go without him.

He was joined at the base shortly after by Stephen and then by Joe.

Each team member had their own gear for the hills for which they received an allowance from the team every year. The local climbing store also gave team members a discount. The gear included boots, ice axe, crampons, helmet, bivouac bag and map and compass. The team supplied each member with a team jersey, a jacket, a GPS receiver and a radio. The stretchers, complete with head guards and snow skis, were already clamped on the roof racks of the two Land Rovers. Alex got out some ropes and a selection of winter climbing gear in case it was required while Stephen switched on the large base radio and then loaded up some casualty bags, a number of large flash lights and checked the first aid kits in the vehicles. Each member of the team carried his own first aid kit but the team kits included a selection of splints, a supply of triangular and other bandages, an intravenous infusion set, cervical collars, morphine, mouth to mouth units, warm air breathing apparatus for the treatment of hypothermia, a vacuum mattress for spinal injuries, Entonox analgesic gas and oxygen.

By this time, other team members were beginning to arrive. Donald, who had retired from the active list after 22 years in the team, would man the base radio in case communication was required beyond the Langdale valley.

As soon, as there were enough team members to fill the first Land Rover, it set off with Alex at the wheel and Joe beside him. As there was no evidence of a snow plough having passed this way recently, Alex slipped it into four wheel drive and drove carefully up the valley with the windscreen wipers working hard against the snow. He switched on the rotating blue light but more out of habit than from any expectation that it would serve much purpose on a night like this.

It was about three quarters of an hour after the call out that the first Land Rover pulled in beside the advanced base at the New Dungeon Ghyll Hotel. In the meantime, David had opened up the advanced base and had switched on the base radio and made contact with Donald at Elterwater. Constable Matthew Harman had arrived at the base about twenty minutes after the call out. Eric was with David and together they told him everything they knew and he passed the gist of this through to Sergeant Williams who was still on his way from Windermere.

Once the team members were inside the hut, Joe asked David and Eric to explain the situation again. They did so, giving a physical description of Jennifer and Stuart, recounting what they had said about their intentions, reporting what they had said about their level of experience and adding that, as of half an hour ago, they had not returned to their tent and were not in the bar at either hotel. While they were doing this the police Land Rover arrived and Sergeant Bill Williams, the police co-ordinator, came in. Bill was well known to a number of the team members and had worked with the team on many rescues. Although the rescue had been initiated by the police, responsibility for running the rescue rested with the team leader. The job of the police co-ordinator was to provide a police presence, to act as liaison with police headquarters and to keep a record of who was doing what and, in particular, who was out on the hills.

Joe turned to the large-scale map on the wall of the hut.

"OK," he said, "I'm sorry to drag you out on New Year's Eve. The weather is going to be unpleasant up on the hills and it may get worse. It looks as though we have enough members to operate in two teams of four and one of five. Please make sure you keep together. There is no point in calling in the helicopter yet; although it can operate at night time, it cannot fly in conditions of zero visibility. I think we should start by covering all the paths. Let's have lots of light and noise. It's going to be difficult in this weather but, as you know, there is more chance of people seeing you than you seeing them. I suggest we send teams up the Band and Rossett Gill. I want another team to go up Hell Gill to Three Tarns and then round Crinkle Crags. The missing pair may have changed their mind about their route when the bad weather arrived. We have only one dog out tonight so Roger would you and Frank take Heinz and I suggest you cover the ground below and around the climbers' traverse, Cambridge Crag and Bowfell Buttress. Has anyone got any other suggestions? Any questions?"

There was a brief discussion about focusing all the resources on the west side of the valley given some uncertainty about the party's destination but it was accepted that that was the most sensible option in the circumstances. Stephen asked what the intentions were once the groups got up on the tops. In these conditions, no one would want to hang around for a discussion. Joe said that his plan at the moment was just to cover the main paths; he would decide what to do after that in the light of conditions and of the way things developed.

"We will need a radio relay set up near Angle Tarn," he added.

Joe then asked Alex to take Chris, Ken and Graham with him up the Band, call sign 'Langdale Alex'. Roger, Frank and Heinz would also start up the Band ahead of them but divert to the ground below the climbers' traverse, call sign 'Dog Roger'. Stephen would take Shelagh, Claire and David up Rossett Gill, call sign 'Langdale Stephen'. Andrew would join them as far as Rossett Gill to operate as radio relay, call sign 'Rossett Relay'. David asked Joe if Eric could join them, given his background and experience; and he mentioned their expedition this morning. Joe agreed and Bill noted him for the record.

Greg offered to drive them to the end of the valley and then return to join one of the other teams once the second Land Rover arrived. They piled into the Land Rover and Greg took them up to the end of the road. Then the Rossett Gill group set off along Mickleden armed with flashlights and head torches and the group going up the Band set off along the track for Stool End Farm similarly armed. Greg took the Land Rover back to the advanced base, arriving at the same time as the second Land Rover with additional team members. Joe repeated his briefing and then Greg took Martin, Richard and Neil and headed for Hell Gill and Three Tarns, call sign 'Langdale Greg.

Back at the advanced base Bill switched on the kettle and made some coffee for himself and Joe. It was going to be a long night.

River Esk, 6.30pm

As she had expected, Lucy had been at no risk of falling asleep. Indeed, the shelter was all but illusory. Although she had been able to rest and warm up a bit in her survival bag, she was fairly exposed and the wind and snow battered the polythene and she wondered if it might tear. After a while, she treated herself to a hot drink from her flask and some mint cake. Then she carefully eased herself out of the survival bag, keeping a tight hold of it so it would not get snatched away by the wind.

"So far, so good," she thought, folding the bag as best she could and stuffing it into her sack. Then using the tussock for support she tried getting onto her feet. The pain in her ankle had eased while she had been resting; but when she tried to put her weight on it, it returned with a vengeance and it was immediately clear that she was not going to walk out.

"Shit!" she said with feeling almost in tears. "Damn! Bloody fucking Hell!" There didn't seem to be any choice but to try crawling. It was clear that, if Peter and the others were to stand any chance, she couldn't stay where she was.

With that she started crawling along on her hands and knees, favouring her injured ankle. The new snow had already settled to some depth and Lucy found herself literally wallowing, almost swimming, through it at times. This, coupled with the occasional boggy patch meant that, notwithstanding her waterproofs, she soon became pretty wet. The process was also very tiring, not to mention sore on the knees. Yet she was making progress, albeit slowly.

After a while, she came to yet another stream coming in from the left. She had no choice but to get up and try and cross on one foot, an exercise which she accomplished but at the price of a boot full of water. She tried hopping as an alternative to crawling but that proved impossible with the combination of the uneven ground and the deep snow. She tried dragging herself along to give some relief to her knees but found that, not only was progress desperately slow, but she was in some danger of being smothered by the snow. Crawling seemed to be the only way forward. She was so focused on what she was doing that she lost all sense of time, she became oblivious to the storm raging around her, she just concentrated on keeping on moving forwards.

Clearly there was a limit to how long she could go on like this. She was beginning to think that perhaps she had reached it when a wall appeared in the feeble beam of her head torch. She stopped to think about this for a moment. Walls can be found all over the Lakeland fells, even up on the tops; so it was not something to get too excited about. Nonetheless, it was the first wall she had seen since they had descended into Eskdale. She thought it probably indicated the edge of the more intensively farmed land. If that was so, she could not be too far from the farm itself. The thought gave her a spur and she decided to get herself on the other side of the wall, make a shelter in the lee, rest for a bit, have some food and drink and study the map.

Getting over the wall was easier said than done. As she had been following a path along the river, she thought there must be a gate or stile nearby. Casting up and down the wall, she eventually found a stile in the form of slabs of stone projecting from the wall. These provided a series of steps but getting onto the steps with one leg was simply not possible. Eventually she managed to hoist herself by kneeling on each step with her bad leg and then using her good leg to stand up. She repeated the exercise to get down the other side. Then she sat down to regain her breath. The relief from the wind was immediately evident and very welcome. She felt an overwhelming urge just to let go and drift off to sleep. It would be so easy and quite painless. She put the thought behind her but decided that a short rest would help as she still had some way to go. With an effort, she reached for her rucksack, dug out her survival bag, eased herself into it, made a pillow with the sack and lay back to rest, determined not to go to sleep

Adam, meanwhile, was reflecting that Lucy should have arrived at the farm by now and would have raised the alarm. He didn't know how long it would take to assemble the rescue team and get them to the farm, perhaps an hour. It might then take them an hour to make their way up the valley. In other words, the earliest they could expect help would be another two hours.

He was not worried about Sam at the moment. She seemed to have revived. She had been quiet for a while but the body warmth from lying so closely together and the comfort of being arm in arm had undoubtedly helped. It was cramped and uncomfortable in the survival bag and movement was strictly limited. It had been impossible to turn over unless Adam heaved himself most of the way out of the bag. They had done that once but it had resulted in a slight tear in the bag and Adam was worried that continued movement would enlarge the tear. The main thing was that they were reasonably warm although Adam had been conscious of cold seeping up from the ground. The wall he had built up from the stones of the old sheep fold had kept out the worst of the weather and most of the snow was piling up against the other side of the wall or was being blown overhead. Nonetheless, some was finding its way onto them and he had to keep clearing it from around their heads.

He was increasingly worried by Peter's condition. They were snuggled up as close against Peter as they could be in order to give him the benefit of their warmth. But there had been no sound from him since he had been put into the survival bag. Adam had tried talking to him and had even tried on a couple of occasions to shake him into a response but to no effect. There was a pulse and so far as Adam could determine in these conditions he seemed to be breathing; but he seemed to have lapsed into a coma. Adam could think of nothing else he could do to help, apart from keeping the snow off his face and praying for the rescue team to arrive in time.

The Band, 8.45pm

Alex kept his team close together going up the Band. He asked Ken to take the lead and to set a steady pace while he brought up the rear. For a while, Roger and Frank with Heinz were ahead of them but they soon diverged from the path. Ken carried one of the flash lights which he switched on from time to time and shone around; but in the driving snow it was unlikely that anyone would see it unless Ken fell over them. Graham carried the other. The team searched any obvious opportunities for shelter on the way up; but apart from that, they trudged on with their heads down against the wind and snow and their head torches providing a feeble beam.

Eventually, when they were somewhere near where he thought the climbers' traverse left the main track, Alex stopped the group. Alex switched on his GPS and checked their position against the map. Then he got on the radio to Control: "Langdale Control, Langdale Control, this is Langdale Alex, do you read me? Over."

"Langdale Alex this is Control, reading you strength five. Over," responded Joe.

Alex gave their position from his GPS receiver. "We are at the junction between the Three Tarns route and the Direct Route up Bowfell. I'm splitting the group to cover both routes. Over."

"What are conditions like? Over," asked Control.

"Blowing force 8 to 9, gusting 10 from the north, driving snow, dark. Over."

"OK," responded Control. "Continue up Bowfell covering both routes then take the Ore Gap to Angle Tarn. Out."

Alex decided to take the direct route with Graham while Chris and Ken would head up to the Three Tarns, both groups to continue to show flash lights. Everyone unstrapped their ice axes from their sacks and Alex shouted instructions about linking up again below the summit of Bowfell. The Three Tarns group were given the temporary call sign 'Langdale Ken'.

Advanced base, 9pm

Back at advanced base, Paul had arrived in time to hear the exchange with Alex.

Bill, the police co-ordinator, suggested it might be worth checking the tent and the bars again. Joe thought it probably would be although he didn't know where the tent was on the site. He radioed Langdale Stephen and asked for an update on their position. He then asked David to explain the location of the tent and the car, which he did. Paul volunteered to go up to the camp site and Constable Matthew Harman accompanied him. They climbed into Paul's van and made their way cautiously up the road.

In the meantime, Joe asked Bill if he could get on to the Met Office and get an update on the forecast for the next twelve hours. The Met Office advised that there would probably be an easing in conditions for a couple of hours towards midnight but that conditions would get worse after that, possibly blowing up to Force 10 or 11, maybe more, on the tops, and not ease off again until well into the next day.

The news from the Met Office caused Joe to think about alerting the rescue helicopter. The Lake District is normally serviced by the rescue helicopter operating out of RAF Bulmer on the Northumberland coast, although contact is made through the Aeronautical Rescue Co-ordination Centre for the UK at RAF Kinloss on the Moray Firth. Provided the chopper is not tied up on RAF business or engaged in another rescue elsewhere, it will respond to a request for assistance from the police if conditions are appropriate. With its powerful searchlights and with the use of night vision goggles, the crew can operate the helicopter at night time. It cannot, however, operate in a white out and given the conditions over the southern fells at present, Joe had not contemplated calling it in. However, the news from the Met Office about a possible window in the weather altered the matter. Joe asked Bill, as police co-ordinator, if he would have a word with the Rescue Co-ordination Centre to check availability. He was told that the Bulmer chopper was currently on standby. Bill explained the position so far regarding the call out including the possibility of a window in the weather, but emphasising that it was not yet certain that there was anyone in need of rescue. Like the mountain rescue teams, the Rescue Co-ordination Centre takes a call out at face value and works on the assumption that there may be someone in need of help.

If it turns out that there is not, well that is good news. Bill said that Control for the rescue had been set up at the New Dungeon Ghyll Hotel in the Langdale Valley, call sign 'Langdale Control'. He was told that he should expect the chopper in about half an hour. Joe switched on a second radio for contact with the chopper and tuned it Channel 1 in the high band.

Meanwhile, Paul and Matthew had found no change at Jennifer and Stuart's tent or at their car. They went across to the Old Dungeon Ghyll bar. The bar was packed with New Year revellers and very noisy. Matthew had to bang for some time on the bar for quiet before he could ask whether the owner of the car was present. This generated some jeering but no other response, so they checked with the hotel itself and then made their way back to the New Dungeon Ghyll. There they checked the bars and the hotel and, again, drew a blank. Then they returned to the base.

Joe put them in the picture regarding the weather and the call to the Rescue Co-ordination Centre and asked them if they could get some flares and standby to guide the chopper down onto the field it normally used when operating in Langdale. Bill said he would slip over and let the hotel manager know what was happening as the field belonged to the hotel.

On his way out Bill collided with the bulky figure of the team doctor who had just arrived. Ben Chapman was a GP in practice in Ambleside. He was a jovial, larger than life character in his late forties with a somewhat avuncular bedside manner. He was an active fell walker but had never climbed in his life. He had been approached about joining the team when the previous team doctor had moved away from the area. He had been a member of the team now for more than ten years and his long-suffering partners had learned long ago that a call out for Ben could mean a call out for them to cover Ben's appointments.

"Who on earth would be mad enough to be out in weather like this?" he boomed shedding water proofs all over the hut floor.

"Well, we are not certain that anyone is," replied Joe and gave him a brief run down on the situation so far. "I don't think there is any point in you going up at this stage," he went on. "If we find someone, then we can see about getting you up there in the chopper." Ben said he wondered if it might be quicker on foot. He recalled one rescue when he had been given a lift down Langdale in the helicopter and the head wind had been so strong that they had been overtaken by the local bus. Joe, who had also been in the helicopter at the time and had been hanging on grimly while the big machine had been knocked around by the wind like a boxer in the ring, responded that if he really wished to walk he was sure no one would stand in his way.

"Meanwhile," said Joe, "how about reviving us all with a mug of coffee."

"Ah now that is the most useful thing I have been asked to do all week," said Ben collecting the kettle.

Rossett Ghyll, 9.30pm

David had never liked Rossett Gill although, with the upgraded track, life is easier than it used to be. The upgrading of the track using inset stones and boulders, essentially a form of cobbling, coupled with surface water drainage is an attempt to stop the erosion in the Gill caused by thousands of booted feet forging their own line. Although the engineered track has been criticised as out of place in this natural landscape and likely to attract ill-equipped walkers into the hills, there is little evidence of this happening; and it does seem to have slowed down the pace of erosion. David thought the track an improvement, except when it is icy at which point the cobbles can be lethal. The track sensibly avoids the direct line up the Gill formerly taken by impatient walkers and climbers. Instead, it follows a zig-zag line corresponding with much of the old pack horse route. Nonetheless, the top part of the Gill, once the track runs out, remains scrambly and unpleasant. This evening they had to cover any possible shelter in the Gill which meant covering both the made-up track and the direct line up the Gill. Stephen asked Shelagh and David to cover the track while he, Andrew, Claire and Eric covered the Gill. Eric carried one of the flash lights which he waved around at intervals. David had another. Stephen kept them at a steady but relentless pace. The only stop was to take the radio call from Control.

They eventually emerged at the top of the Gill at about 9.30pm to be greeted by a blast of wind and snow funnelling through the gap. They had to push hard to make headway against it. The wind tunnel effect eased a bit as they left the gap and dropped down towards Angle Tarn. Stephen contacted control and requested instructions. Joe asked them to check out the path heading north east from Angle Tarn behind Rossett Pike towards the top of the Stake Pass. They had a glimpse of the tarn itself through the snow and then they were plodding up towards the back of Rossett Pike. Eric shone the flashlight around but it is doubtful whether it would have been visible at more than ten metres.

Andrew decided to set up the radio relay in a relatively sheltered spot on the rising ground below Rossett Pike. The team radios are very efficient but it is still not possible to bend radio waves around or over mountains so that relays have to be used to maintain contact once teams are out of line of sight with Control. In this case, contact with Control would be problematic once Langdale Stephen got behind Rossett Pike and once Langdale Alex came off the summit of Bowfell into the Ore Gap – hence the relay. Andrew reported in to Control that Rossett Relay was now established and gave the map reference from his GPS receiver.

Crinkle Crags, 9.30pm

While Langdale Alex and Langdale Stephen were working their way up the Band and Rossett Gill respectively, Langdale Greg had been struggling through deep snow in Oxendale. At the point where the footbridge crosses Oxendale Beck, Langdale Greg turned up towards Hell Gill. The waterfall below Hell Gill was muted with the volume of snow. The Gill, itself, is a steep sided gorge and the team took some time working their way up it checking it out. There was no sign of anyone having been that way and they returned to climb the steep track beside the Gill that follows Buscoe Sike towards Three Tarns.

Advanced base, 9.50pm

"Langdale Control, Langdale Control, this is Rescue 57, do you read? Over," crackled the second radio.

Joe reached for the transmitter. "Rescue 57 this is Langdale Control reading you strength 4. Over."

"We are passing over Kendal and should be with you in about five minutes. What are the conditions like in Langdale valley? Over."

"The wind has eased to about Force 7 from the north and shows signs of decreasing further. Visibility has improved to about 500 metres. It has been snowing hard but that too is showing signs of easing. Over."

"Oh, that's what it is on the windscreen, I was wondering!" responded Rescue 57. "In view of conditions, we will land at advanced base. Over."

Joe grinned, "Roger that. Do you want flares at the landing field?"

"Affirmative," responded Rescue 57, although whether he would be able to see them in these conditions until he was over the field was doubtful thought the pilot.

Joe ended the exchange. Paul and Matthew put on their jackets and water proof trousers and made their way out to the field beside the hotel. They stood on the down wind side some distance apart and waited. It wasn't long before they heard the clattering of the helicopter above the noise of the wind so they lit their flares. Bright orange smoke streamed off down the valley.

"Ahh,", murmured Paul.

The pilot switched on the machine's landing lights as they approached the field. In view of the poor visibility, they did not immediately see the flares. When they were right over head, the pilot slowly descended through the snow. The reflection off the snow made for poor visibility and this was not helped by the maelstrom of new snow whipped up by the huge rotor blades as the machine slowly descended. The crew man had the door open and was helping to guide the pilot down while the pilot kept a close eye on his radio altimeter. Eventually, the big Sea King settled onto the field. The pilot kept the rotor blades turning until fully satisfied of the stability of his position and then he shut the engines down. What seemed for a moment like silence descended on the valley. Eventually, the crew of four climbed out encumbered in flying gear.

Paul made his way across and shouted for the crew to follow him to the base. The Elterwater team had worked together with the chopper on numerous rescues, they had practised together and they had even socialised together. Paul's head still ached when he thought of the dinner dance at Bulmer that he had attended with other members of the team in the summer.

"Come in, it's good to see you," said Paul as they arrived at the hut.

"I wish I could say the same," responded the pilot, Flight Lieutenant Ron Corfield, "You have some foul weather here."

"Well, I realise you don't like getting your helicopter wet," retorted

Paul, "so we have laid on some better weather for you – relatively speaking."

"Yes, I was hearing about that on the way over," said Ron, "If we are lucky, I think we should be able to get up for about two hours."

Ron Corfield and his co-pilot, Sean, and the crew man, Dave, were known to those in the hut from previous rescues. The navigator, Flight Lieutenant Tony Beaumont, was new and there were introductions all round. Joe then explained the situation so far.

Bowfell, 9.30pm

Meanwhile, with some help from the radio and much flashing of lights, 'Langdale Alex' and 'Langdale Ken' had managed to re-establish contact below the summit of Bowfell. The flash lights illuminated the snow encrusted figures, the wind tearing frantically at the waterproof clothing, and the whirling snow. From there they continued up onto the summit. At 2,960 feet, Bowfell is the highest mountain in the Langdale circuit. It was also a very inhospitable mountain that night. The wind was tearing across the summit blowing the snow horizontally into their faces. Alex thought it must be blowing at well over 50 mph. Heading into it was like trying to push a car uphill. Shouting at the group to keep close together and to try and keep an eye open for anything unusual, Alex didn't stop but took off on a bearing towards the Ore Gap. He had pre-programmed the route into his GPS and used this as an additional check from the summit. He had no intention of getting tangled up in Hanging Knotts crag if he could avoid it. It was slow going straight into the teeth of the gale. The only consolation was that they were heading gradually downhill again. It nonetheless required a concentrated effort and there was no prospect of turning aside to check out boulders and humps. If the couple they were looking for had gone to ground in the summit area, the prospects of survival were slim indeed.

The team were quite tired and feeling decidedly battered by the time they started to descend through the Gap. Alex thought the wind was dying down a bit. It was still blowing hard but not with the same intensity as they had experienced on the top. He didn't allow himself to become too hopeful. It might just be the consequence of dropping some 600 feet. However, as they made their way through the Gap, it became clear that conditions were easing. The snow was no longer driving horizontally at them. When they joined the path from Esk Hause, Alex linked up with Control via Rossett Relay to explain the change.

Joe responded that the Met Office had forecast an easing of conditions for an hour or two. In view of the change, he asked Alex to have a careful look around Angle Tarn and would give further instructions after that.

Meanwhile, in Langdale Stephen team members had begun to feel the benefit of the improved conditions as they skirted Rossett Crag and headed towards Black Crags. It had been slow going as they were heading straight into the wind; but with the easing of the wind they could now communicate without shouting all the time.

Langdale Greg had by this time emerged from Hell Gill and Buscoe Sike and arrived at Three Tarns. Greg reported into Control and was asked, in view of the window in the weather, to take their time checking out Crinkle Crags.

Rescue 57, 10.10pm

Ron and Sean had gone outside to get a feel for the changing conditions. In the valley the wind had died down to a breeze and the snow had almost stopped. It was impossible to see the cloud base from where they were but there was a chance that that too might have lifted a bit.

"Right," said Ron, "I think we should give it a try. If the forecast is correct we haven't got long."

They returned to the hut and discussed with Joe what they could most usefully do in the relatively short time they were likely to have available. As the teams were covering the paths and the tops, Joe thought a sweep along the crags of Bowfell and the Crinkles, particularly the bottom of the crags, would be helpful. The forward looking infra-red equipment carried by the machine could pick out heat spots which might indicate a missing walker – but might equally indicate a sheep. If conditions did not permit a search of the crags, then a sweep of the Mickleden and Oxendale valleys would be useful.

Joe suggested that Paul and Ben should go along as well so they could be dropped off if anything seemed worth investigating. Ben said he could think of nothing he would rather be doing. Joe also asked Ron if he could take two of the team stretchers on board, together with some additional rescue gear in case they needed to be dropped off. Collecting their gear, Paul and Ben made their way to the chopper and clambered aboard. Dave, the crew man strapped them in. Ron and Sean went through their pre-flight checks and then Ron started up the engines and the machine rose from the field, tilted forward slightly and headed off down Mickleden towards Bowfell.

Sean noted that the head wind was already down to less than 20 knots. As the snow had more or less stopped, Ron, Sean and Dave were wearing night vision goggles and the surrounding countryside appeared green to them but reasonably clear. Dave had the door open as they flew along and was kneeling beside it looking out. Tony was seated sideways behind the pilots hunched over his navigation equipment. Paul and Ben were strapped in next to Dave. Paul shouted over the noise of the engine to ask if there were any spare goggles. Dave produced a spare set and Paul manoeuvred himself so he could see out. Ben was content to sit where he was.

Ron kept the search lights off while they wore night vision goggles. He flew high enough above Mickleden so as not to disturb the ground with the down wash from the rotor blades and took his time. This enabled Sean, Dave and Paul to have a good look. Paul was impressed to note how much more ground they could visually search with the advantage of a bit of height. Even so, the new snow was going to make it difficult to spot anything unusual.

When he arrived above the sheepfold at the end of Mickleden, Ron headed for Rossett Gill and the Sea King rose slowly up towards the cloud base which had lifted to about 2,500 feet. Keeping just below the cloud base, Ron turned south and began to fly along parallel to the crags that make up the east face of Bowfell. He hovered opposite the bottom of Bowfell Buttress so that they could check the climbers' traverse and the boulder slope between the buttress and Cambridge Crag.

Roger and Frank had seen the helicopter approaching as they worked their way along the track which links the climbers' traverse from Bowfell Buttress to Rossett Gill. They had initially covered the slope below the traverse and then Heinz had energetically searched the boulder slopes beside Cambridge Crag and Bowfell Buttress while Roger and Frank made their way along the traverse towards Rossett Gill. When the helicopter came past, they turned into the slope and put an arm over their faces as the down draught spun the snow up around them. Then the machine was passed and they continued towards the Gill. By Bowfell Links above Three Tarns, Ron turned the machine round, dropped some 500 feet and traversed back along Bowfell towards Rossett Gill. This time the helicopter passed by beneath Roger and Frank.

River Esk, 10.15pm

Lucy woke up with a start. For a moment she was totally disorientated. However, as her memory returned she frantically switched on her head torch and checked her watch. It showed just after 10.15pm. She was horrified. She was supposed to be going for help. Adam, Sam and Peter were relying on her and yet here she was tucked behind a wall fast asleep. Apart from the gut-wrenching feeling of guilt, Lucy had to admit she felt better for the sleep. The weather also seemed to have eased. The wind had dropped to a breeze and the snow was still falling but in an almost leisurely fashion. Perhaps things would turn out all right after all, she thought. She thought enviously of the New Year revellers who would be gathering in the warmth of the Old Dungeon Ghyll Hotel. She opened her flask and treated herself to half a cup of luke warm fruit juice and some chocolate. While she was drinking, she checked the map and identified what she thought might be the wall she was sheltering behind. Then she eased herself out of her survival bag and packed it away in her rucksack. She was still unable to stand on her injured foot, so with a quick check of her compass, she started crawling across the field. Her knees were swollen and sore from her earlier efforts and restarting was excruciatingly painful. Her initial reaction was that she couldn't do it; it was too much to expect of her. After lying in the snow for a bit, she tried again. It was just as painful but, as she was expecting it, it didn't seem quite so bad. She gritted her teeth and made her way slowly across the field. After a while, the knees became numb and the pain merged into the general background of total discomfort.

She was careful to keep the river on her right hand side as she crawled along; the last thing she wanted was to be going round in circles in the dark. Eventually, she came to another wall. Again, she cast around for a gate or stile and, again, she found a stile comprising stones embedded in the wall. Her recent experience enabled her to surmount this one with a minimum of effort and it was not long before she found herself on the other side of the wall. Hesitantly, she lowered herself onto her knees and gingerly made her way forward again.

The next hurdle she encountered was another stream coming in from the right. Cursing, she sat down at the edge of it and wondered how long she could go on. Well, there was only one way to find out. She could see no way of avoiding a wet foot this time; there was no convenient flat stone in the middle to hop on to and it was too far across to make it in one hop. So she placed her foot as far into the stream as she could. The cold water pouring in over the top of her boot made her gasp. Then she pushed herself up onto the foot and fell across to the far side and hauled herself out. She decided that if she stopped now she would just burst into tears so she pressed on. Yet another wall appeared in the dim light of her head torch and she broke into a stream of invective. Swearing seemed to relieve some of her tension but it had no effect on the wall so, again, she looked around for some means to cross it. This time she found a ladder stile and slowly dragged herself up and over it. Then it was down onto her knees and on again.

She didn't notice the building until she was almost past it. For a moment it didn't sink in. Then she realised it was a complex of build-ings and that she must at long last have arrived in the farmyard. She lay there for a moment enjoying the prospect of the end of her ordeal. Then she crawled on looking for the farmhouse which was part of the complex. She made her way slowly over to the front door adding a quantity of slur-ry to the mud on her waterproofs and hauled herself up on to her good leg. She looked for a bell but couldn't see one. Instead, she hammered hard on the door with the small brass knocker. There was no response. She tried again, and again; but to no avail. It slowly dawned on her that there was no one at home. There were no lights to be seen and no car in the yard. It was all too much. She sat down on the doorstep and burst into tears.

Further back up Eskdale Adam was getting increasingly worried. He had expected the rescue team to appear about an hour ago. He wondered if Lucy had managed to get through. He thought Peter was dead. He seemed to have slipped imperceptibly from life to death sometime dur-ing the last hour. He did not seem to be breathing and Adam was unable to detect any pulse; but, as he was not sure where and how he should be checking for this, he could not be entirely sure.

Sam's condition was also beginning to worry him. Although they were both reasonably warm and although he could see in the light of his head torch that she was still breathing, she had relapsed into a sort of stupor during the last hour and he had been unable to rouse her, although he had not tried very hard.

He had noticed the improvement in the weather and had wondered whether he and Sam should try and make a break for it down the valley – if he could rouse her. Had he been sure that Peter was dead, he would have removed his wind proofs and jersey and put them on Sam; but he felt he couldn't do so while he was still uncertain.

He decided to wait another half hour and then decide.

Angle Tarn, 11pm

"Langdale Control, Langdale Control, this is Rossett Relay, do you read? Over"

Joe reached for the transmitter. "Rossett Relay, this is Control. Reading you strength 5. Pass your message. Over."

"Control, Langdale Alex have found a casualty below Hanging Knotts Crag. The position is GR 246075. Over".

Joe had heard similar messages many times but he still found it electrifying. The short message changed the whole nature of the exercise from a search for a possible casualty to the rescue of an actual casualty. It also vindicated his strategy for the search. He knew Langdale Alex would be experiencing mixed feelings: satisfaction that their efforts had come to something but sadness that someone had, indeed, come to grief. He heard later how the discovery had been made.

The struggle up to and across the summit of Bowfell in such difficult conditions had taken quite a lot out of the team members in Langdale Alex. Once they had got down near Angle Tarn, Alex had found a sheltered spot behind some boulders and had given them a ten-minute break. They had all had a warm drink from their flasks and a bite to eat. While they were there, Roger and Frank with Heinz had appeared at the top of Rossett Gill and made their way down to the tarn. Alex had asked Roger and Frank with Heinz to search the slope immediately to the west and south of Angle Tarn and below Hanging Knotts Crag while he searched down by the tarn. Meanwhile, he asked Ken and Chris to work their way round the north and east side of the tarn covering both sides of the footpath. He had everyone spread out so as to cover as much of the ground as possible.

The snow was soft and quite deep and to avoid the prospect of a slide down towards Angle Tarn, it had been necessary for Roger and Frank on the hillside below Hanging Knotts to stamp down the snow to ensure a footing. Frank had prospected around the bottom of the crag with a flashlight in hand while Roger and Heinz had taken a line across the middle of the slope. Alex, meantime, had approached from the other side searching lower down along shore of the tarn.

Heinz had not been enthusiastic about conditions so far. His hair was heavily matted with lumps of ice and he was generally feeling that he had had enough of a walk for one evening. He had needed some encouragement to diverge from the path and onto the slope below Hanging Knotts. However, he had begun to show signs first of all of alertness and then of excitement as he and Roger had worked across the slope. Roger realised he had acquired a scent. Heinz had gone on ahead almost paddling through the snow to a large snow covered boulder and had begun prancing around and barking. Roger had made his way over and found what looked like a snow covered body lying tucked in behind the boulder. He had shouted to the others and had started clearing the snow off the clothing and face. Heinz had been keen to help but in his enthusiasm he had ended up covering up more than he had cleared and he eventually had to be shooed away. He had moved back a few paces and had sat there looking hurt. Alex had come up to join Roger and they had carried out a quick check for vital signs but with no obvious success. Whoever it was did not seem to be breathing and Alex had been unable to detect a pulse. Alex had sent a message via Rossett Relay informing Control of the finding.

"Rossett Relay, the chopper will bring the team doctor and other teams will be redirected to Angle Tarn," said Joe. "Alex is to take charge at the site. Let me know the status of the casualty and any identification when you can. Out."

Joe radioed the chopper and asked it to take Ben, Paul and the stretchers and other gear to Angle Tarn and then to collect Langdale Greg from Crinkle Crags and uplift them to Angle Tarn. Langdale Stephen were asked to turn back from Rossett Crag to Angle Tarn. Langdale Greg were asked to find a suitable spot for a helicopter pick up and to pass the GPS position to Control for onward transmission to the chopper.

Meanwhile, Alex and Ken undertook a thorough assessment of the casualty's condition. They were still unable to detect any vital signs but Alex knew that with cold casualties, and this one was very cold, that did not necessarily mean they were dead. There had been cases of mountaineers caught out in winter conditions and showing no vital signs, being revived in hospital. Nonetheless, there was no detectable pulse, the casualty did not seem to be breathing and the pupils of the eyes were dilated and unresponsive to light. The head injuries were evident and serious, although with the cold there had not been much bleeding. There was a substantial gash at the base of the skull and Alex thought he could detect a fracture. It was difficult to determine what other breakages there might be. The back and pelvis seemed intact. Alex was not sure about the ribs. The left leg was out of alignment and was almost certainly broken. The distribution of injuries suggested the casualty had tumbled on his way down.

Ken searched the pockets and found a wallet which indicated that the casualty was a Stuart Morris, apparently a student from Sheffield. Alex realised this was one of the two missing people they were looking for. That meant that the other was probably somewhere in the vicinity. He asked Chris and Graham to check out the slope round about and to investigate the bottom of Hanging Knotts Crag. He also asked them to keep an eye open for Stuart's rucksack. Roger meantime had to take time out to reassure Heinz that he was indeed the cleverest dog in the world but that, as such, he shouldn't be making quite so much fuss. Heinz, feeling neglected after the excitement of the find, had been leaping about and barking to attract attention.

"Control, this is Rossett Relay. Over."

"Pass your message Rossett Relay," responded Joe.

"Casualty critical. Hypothermia, head and other serious injuries. Vital signs very weak. Alex requests immediate helicopter evacuation. Identification suggests this is Stuart Morris." Andrew spelt out the name.

Joe understood the reference to 'very weak' vital signs. There was a standing instruction that a police officer must attend the scene of a death so as to examine the location. But, like Alex, he had heard of cases where winter casualties, although showing no vital signs, had subsequently been revived. However, time was of the essence and any delay while a police officer was brought up to examine the scene could be fatal.

There was a tendency to play safe in such situations and avoid reference to 'no vital signs'.

There was a further consideration. Team members had been out in severe conditions and it was not desirable to keep them out any longer than was absolutely necessary. He needed to get them down, if possible before the window in the weather closed. Joe agreed with Alex's request for a helicopter evacuation and said he would speak to the chopper.

Bill, who had been listening to the exchange, said that Stuart Morris was the name of one of the two they were looking for. The question was where was the girl.

Joe got on to Rescue 57 first and explained the request for a helicopter evacuation if Ron thought it could be achieved, Ron to liaise directly with Alex at the scene, call sign Langdale Alex. Then he radioed Rossett Relay.

"Control, this is Rossett Relay," Andrew replied. "Pass your message. Over."

"Rossett Relay, tell Alex to communicate direct with the chopper over the evacuation. When the other teams arrive ask Alex to arrange a local search for Jennifer Halliwell, the companion of Stuart Morris. Over."

"Roger, Control. Out to you". "Langdale Alex, this is Rossett Relay. Over".

"Rossett Relay, this is Langdale Alex, pass your message. Over."

Andrew passed on the request from Control for a local search for the second person. Roger, who was now handling the radio for Langdale Alex, acknowledged. He borrowed a second radio and switched it to channel 1 on the high band for communication with the chopper.

Alex and Ken, meanwhile, had bandaged Stuart's head as best as they were able and had splinted his legs together. Then they had put him into a bivouac bag to try and maintain whatever warmth remained.

At that point, an increasing volume of noise heralded the arrival of the Sea King which made its appearance through the gap at the head of Rossett Gill. The noise reverberated around the bowl in which Angle Tarn lies and Alex looked anxiously up at the cliffs of Hanging Knotts hoping that it would not trigger an avalanche of new snow. Ron headed for the flattish area near the entry to the Ore Gap. Removing the night vision goggles he switched on his landing lights and also the search lights and hovered while the crew got accustomed to the change and had a good look at the terrain. For the rescue team, the powerful lights seemed to turn night into day. Then Ron slowly lowered the chopper to the point where two of the wheels touched down on the uneven ground. Dave waved to Ben and Paul to exit the aircraft and then he passed out the stretchers and other gear. Sean, the co-pilot, advised Langdale Alex that the chopper was going on to collect Langdale Greg and Ron immediately took off and headed up over the summit of Bowfell.

As the chopper lights were extinguished, the hillside was plunged back into darkness apart from the occasional flashlight and the bobbing head torches like so many glow worms. Everyone's night vision was totally wrecked for the moment. As the clatter of the rotor blades receded, silence returned and the immensity of the night reasserted itself.

Ben and Paul arrived carrying the two halves of one of the stretchers. Alex briefed Ben on what they had found and on what they had done so far. Ben opened his rucksack and got out his stethoscope and then, with Ken's assistance, examined Stuart. Paul assembled the stretcher.

After a while Ben stood up. "No, I'm afraid it doesn't look good. We need to get him out as quickly as we can."

"Right," said Alex, "let's get him onto the vacuum mattress for full body immobilisation and then into a casualty bag and onto the stretcher." Ben supervised the use of the team's only vacuum mattress and then Paul and Ken helped Ben to zip Stuart into the casualty bag while Alex manoeuvred the stretcher along side. The four of them lifted the casualty onto the stretcher and strapped him down.

Alex reported via the Relay to Control on the position so far. Then he looked up the slope to where Chris and Graham were probing along the bottom of Hanging Knotts Crag.

"What do you think?" he said to Paul.

"Well, given his position behind this boulder, my guess would be a fall down the gully above us on Hanging Knotts Crag."

"Yes, my thoughts exactly. The question is whether the girl is up there in the gully or whether she also fell and is down here somewhere covered over by the snow; or perhaps she saw her partner fall and went back up to the safety of the summit area of Bowfell and is sheltering up there somewhere. Once Langdale Greg and Langdale Stephen arrive, I'll organise a sweep search of the area between the bottom of the crags and

Angle Tarn; and I'll get Stephen to take a look at the gully. He's our most experienced snow and ice climber. Meantime, we'll stand by to load the stretcher on to the chopper when it returns. We need to move fast on this because the bad weather is supposed to be returning with a vengeance."

Paul asked whether it would be possible for the chopper to check the crag, particularly the gully, with its searchlights and infra red equipment first in case there was anything to be seen. Alex weighed up the need to evacuate Stuart as quickly as possible against the urgent need to find the girl. Overall, he thought the extra minutes involved in a quick check of the gully would be justified.

At that point Langdale Stephen appeared from the direction of Rossett Crag. Alex explained the position to Stephen and asked him about checking out the gully. Stephen agreed and asked David if he would give him a hand. He knew David had done a certain amount of snow and ice climbing and the two of them had climbed together before. Stephen collected one of the team climbing ropes and they sorted out some climbing gear, put on helmets and strapped on their crampons.

Shortly after, a tremendous racket announced the return of the helicopter. It reappeared over the summit of Bowfell and dropped down towards level ground near the Ore Gap. The lights came on again and Ron spent a little while examining the ground before cautiously lowering the machine onto its wheels on a flattish area. The rotor blades kept turning as Langdale Greg piled out.

Alex advised Ron by radio that the stretcher was ready for evacuation and that Ben would like to accompany it. He mentioned that, in view of the identity of the casualty, they were now looking for a second person who may also have been involved in a fall in the gully and requested a quick check of the gully with the searchlights and infra red equipment before the stretcher was uplifted. Ron hesitated before agreeing. The benefits of quickly locating a casualty were obvious. Against that, he was conscious of the wide sweep of his rotor blades in such a confined area and was uncomfortable about hovering near cliff faces in such unpredictable conditions. However, he thought it likely they would get some advance indication of the return of the storm which would allow him to get clear; and at present it was still relatively calm. He lifted off and headed across to Hanging Knotts Crag.

Stephen and David were ready to head for the gully but stayed back while the chopper probed the crag with its searchlights. The combination of the noise from the engines and the action of the rotor blades was loosening the snow on the crag and causing it to swirl up into its own localised storm. A fair amount of it came cascading down onto the slope at the foot of the cliff. Because of this, the crew of the chopper were having difficulty seeing the detail of the gully very clearly. Sean thought there might be something at the point where the rock wall jutted out into the gully about just over a third of the way up and this seemed to be supported by the infra red equipment but they could not be sure. Sean reported this to Langdale Alex while Ron was debating whether to manoeuvre for a closer look.

Ron had just decided that the risk of a closer look was too great because of the fickleness of the weather when a fierce gust of wind heralded the return of the blizzard. A Sea King helicopter weighs around ten tons. The gust nonetheless caught it sideways on and tossed it towards the cliff so that the rotor blades were now perilously close to Hanging Knotts Crag. Ron reacted instinctively by applying more power from the twin turbines. This had the effect of increasing the collective pitch of the rotor blades and lifting the aircraft. In the same movement, Ron tilted the rotor blades to move the machine sideways away from the cliff. Then he swung the helicopter round thus reducing the surface area exposed to the force of the wind. Tilting the rotor blades forwards moved the machine away from the cliff at the same time as a second massive gust hit them. For a moment the machine shuddered and seemed to stop in its tracks. Then, as the gust died away, the turbines carried the machine up and away from the cliff.

Sean, in the co-pilot's seat, found he had been holding his breath. He had been sure they were going to hit the cliff. He wondered whether he would have reacted so fast had he been in control. "For a moment that was quite exciting," he observed nervously.

With the battering of the gale throughout the afternoon and the constant cold, Jennifer had eventually drifted into a stupor and from there into unconsciousness. The bright lights and the shocking noise dragged her back to semi-consciousness and came to her through a sort of fog. Somehow they seemed distant and unreal. She lay there floating. Then they receded and the fog overwhelmed her again and she sank back into unconsciousness.

Sean got on the radio to Alex.

"Langdale Alex, Langdale Alex, this is Rescue 57. Over."

"Rescue 57, this is Langdale Alex. Pass your message. Over."

"It looks as though the window in the weather is over. If the stretcher is ready, we will winch it up; the hillside is too steep to load it directly into the machine. Then we will return to base. Because of the conditions, we will not, repeat not, winch up the doctor. Over."

"Roger that, Rescue 57. For a moment there I thought you were going to give us some additional business. Out," responded Langdale Alex.

Alex cleared the hillside in the vicinity of the stretcher while Paul arranged the lifting straps. Ron brought the machine in to hover over the slope. The whole exercise would need to be accomplished quickly. The danger would be if the machine was hit by another gust while the stretcher was being winched up. Dave as winch man was immediately lowered to arrange the lift. Dave quickly checked the straps, then attached the stretcher and himself to the wire. On his signal, the stretcher and Dave were winched up and the stretcher was in process of being secured when a further gust hit the machine. Ron had the helicopter facing into the wind so that, although it staggered, it retained its position until Dave indicated that all was secure.

The wind, meanwhile, settled down into a steady gale and the snow returned. With windscreen wipers working hard, Ron lifted the machine until the altimeter showed a comfortable margin between themselves and the summit of Bowfell. After a radio exchange with Control he turned south and headed for Lancaster Hospital to unload the casualty. A strong tail wind hurried them on their way, almost as if they were being chased away from the mountains.

Meanwhile, back on the ground Alex started to organise the team into a line for a sweep search of the ground below Hanging Knotts Crag while Stephen and David climbed up to the foot of the gully and the storm closed in around them again.

Brotherilkeld Farm, 11.15 pm

Lucy's first reaction after the overwhelming disappointment of the empty farm house was to find some way of breaking into the house or the barn to take shelter. There might be a phone in the house she could use.

However, respect for people and property was ingrained and she found she could not contemplate just putting a brick through a window. The batteries of her head torch were on their last legs but in the dim light she could just pick out on the map the symbol for a telephone at the junction of the track from the farm with the public road over Hard Knott Pass. There must be a public call box at the junction from which she could call the emergency services. With very considerable reluctance she committed herself to crawling the few hundred yards down to the road. The pain in her knees was agony and she was sorely tempted to give up and find refuge in the barn. However, she managed to half crawl and half drag herself along the track until eventually the outline of the kiosk appeared out of the darkness right on the junction of the farm track with the road.

She paused for a moment for a rest and then hauled herself onto her sound foot. It was one of the old substantial red kiosks. The door took some opening as the snow had piled up against it but eventually she got it partially open and squeezed inside. Her torch had given out so she had to feel for the phone in the dark. It took her some time for her brain to work out what her hands were telling her. Eventually, however, she understood. There was no phone. The kiosk had been vandalised and all that was left was the container and some wires. For a moment she was too shocked to react. Then she gave up.

Lingcove Beck, 11.30 pm

Adam found he was increasingly checking his watch. He had let half an hour go by but still there was no sign of rescue. With the improvement in the weather he had been expecting someone to show up some time ago. He had been turning over and over in his mind the choices open to him. The more he thought about it the more he was coming round to the conclusion that something must have happened to Lucy to prevent her calling out the rescue team. It was possible that someone on the camp site would eventually realise that a party had not returned to their tent. They had said 'good morning' to a couple of lads in the tent next to them that morning; but with the comings and goings over the New Year weekend, it might be days before anyone raised the alarm. Peter had left a note on the car windscreen but that was presumably hidden by snow and would remain so until it thawed. No, the sensible option was to go for help himself.

The next question was what to do about Sam. He had got no response from her for sometime and he didn't think that, even if he could rouse her, she would be in any state to try walking out. She would impede his progress and slow down the whole process of rescue. However, he ought to see whether he could bring her round and explain the position; it would be awful if she came to and found him gone. He also wondered if there was anything he could do to maintain her body warmth. He recognised that the two of them together in the survival bag had generated a considerable amount of warmth and that removing himself could put Sam at risk. On the other hand, they had got steadily colder as time had passed and unless help arrived soon, she would simply slip quietly away like Peter.

Adam thought that, as some compensation, he would leave Sam his own jumper. He had his waterproof jacket and, with the combination of the easing of the weather and the warmth generated by walking, that should be sufficient for him. He could also take Peter's jumper and pass that to Sam. Peter wouldn't be needing it anymore and Adam was sure he would have wanted him to do what he could for Sam. Perhaps he could also take Peter's survival bag and put it under Sam to protect her from the cold seeping up through. He wondered whether he was being callous and would be criticised by the rescue team. It seemed unreal that he was having to make life and death decisions when only a few hours before all four of them had been in a happy holiday mood. Well, he had had no training for this sort of situation so he could only do what he thought was best in the circumstances. He found he didn't much mind if he was criticised, just so long as Sam survived.

He cleared the snow from their survival bag and then shook Sam and called her name. There was no response. He tried again but without success. He got out his thermos and poured the last of the warm fruit juice into the cup and holding her head in his arm tried to get her to drink. He spilled quite a lot but some went in and she choked and opened her eyes. He took his time giving her the remains of the juice and some chocolate while she came round. Then he explained what he intended to do. He wasn't sure if Sam understood. He had expected some resistance from her to being left on her own; but she just lay there looking vacant. He went through it a second time but to no effect. Then he stripped off his jumper and, with difficulty, eased Sam's jacket off, put on the additional jumper and then restored her jacket.

Then he went over to Peter and checked as thoroughly as he could for vital signs. He found none. With a struggle, he pulled the survival bag from him and placed it underneath Sam. Then he removed Peter's jacket and jumper. Although both were wet, the jumper was made of wool and could still generate warmth even though wet. He thought it might be best if Sam wore the jumper like thermal underpants. He helped her to unzip and remove her waterproof trousers; but getting her boots and trousers off was altogether too much of an effort. So she pulled the jumper up over her trousers instead and then put the waterproof trousers back on. Finally, with Adam's help, she put Peter's windproof jacket on top of hers. It hampered her ability to move and she had to be helped back into the survival bag. With all the clothing, she looked very much like the Michelin man in the tyre advertisement; but Adam thought it should help to retain warmth.

Adam collected all the remaining food, along with Peter's thermos and his head torch and placed them within easy reach. Sam's own head torch still had quite a lot of life as she had not been using it since they had gone to ground. Then he used Peter's rucksack to make her a more comfortable head rest. Finally, he gave her a kiss and a hug and with a quick check of the compass he set off into the night.

CHAPTER 5

Angle Tarn, just after midnight, New Year's Day

David was wishing he hadn't agreed to help Stephen in the gully. He was belayed at the bottom and the wind and the snow were driving straight at him. It must be blowing a full force 9 gale he thought with winds around 50 mph. Stephen was about 70 feet up. He had cleared away what seemed like a ton of new snow on his way up so as to secure a safe footing in the hard packed snow underneath and the laws of gravity had ensured that David received most of what he discarded. He now looked very much like an ungainly snowman. He looked gloomily down at what little he could see through the snow of the sweep search which was working its way slowly across the slope beneath.

Stephen had taken his time with the climb and had managed to place a couple of runners on the way up and he was now looking for somewhere to belay before bringing David up. When it was David's turn to climb, he attached an additional rope to his harness in case they needed to haul up equipment and then cramponed up the steep slope with the aid of two short-handled ice axes. His sack was heavy with the addition of a large first aid kit but there was no technical difficulty in the climb and the clearance of the new snow meant he was able to join Stephen very quickly. He tied in to his belay mindful of the lesson he had learned on Gimmer Crag yesterday and Stephen climbed on.

About ten feet above the belay, the rock wall seemed to project prominently into the gully providing an overhang that appeared to bar the way to further progress.

"There seems to be a crack on the right hand side of the overhang and I'm going to try and get some protection into it," said Stephen. "Just be ready to hold me if necessary. It looks decidedly dodgy."

With those encouraging words, he worked his way slowly up towards the overhang clearing new snow all the way and creating an additional private blizzard for David's exclusive enjoyment. He spent some time clearing out the crack before trying to wedge a piece of iron-mongery into it from the selection on his climbing harness. After several tries, he was eventually satisfied with his runner and clipped the rope into the snap link at the end of it and tugged experimentally. It held and Stephen was then able to turn his attention to surmounting the overhang. It was quickly clear to him that it could not be climbed directly so he turned back to the crack. On investigation the crack turned out to be a gap between the projecting rock forming the overhang and the far wall of the gully. The gap widened further up and by pulling up on his runner Stephen was able to reach up and jam his hand firmly into the crack. Kicking the front points of his right crampon high into the wall of the gully, he hauled himself grunting and swearing up and over the overhang into a sort of elbow in the gully. Immediately after, he called down to say he had found someone.

There was a delay while he looked around for somewhere to belay himself securely.

"Does whoever it is have red hair?" David shouted up.

There was a pause, then: "Yes, she does."

"OK, that sounds like the person we are looking for." David radioed down to Alex to let him know and he passed the message to Control via the relay. The sweep search was stopped and the team began to make their way up the slope to the bottom of the gully.

After a while Stephen called down: "She's unconscious but I think she is still alive. I'm belayed securely. If I bring you up, see if you can find yourself a secure stance in the gully just above the projecting rock."

David recovered the belaying gear from his stance and climbed on up to the overhang. Stephen had him on a tight rope while he had a look at the position. There seemed to be enough room for him above the overhang; and a search with the head torch revealed the prospect of a good belay in a crack in the gully wall on the opposite side to and some way above Stephen. David followed Stephen's lead in pulling on the runner and jamming his hand high in the crack and then heaving himself up over the overhang. After a bit of gardening with the pick of his axe, David managed to fix up a satisfactory anchor. Then he cleared away a stance so that he could stand in the gully in reasonable comfort.

Jennifer was lying unconscious in an orange plastic survival bag cradled in the elbow formed by the projection of rock. That at least seemed encouraging. It could be that she had had sufficient command of her senses after the accident to get herself into the survival bag. Of course, it could equally be the case that Stuart had helped her into the bag and had then fallen while going for help. Stephen meanwhile had managed to slip a belaying sling around her chest and had attached her to the cliff and now, true to form, was industriously clearing away the new snow around her. They could detect a pulse although it was weak and she seemed to be breathing, although her breathing was shallow. David tried calling her name several times but there was no response.

Their objective was to get her out of the gully as quickly as possible and clearly going down offered a better option than going up. However, before they could consider moving her, they needed to check for injuries. Normally this would be done by feeling for abnormalities which might indicate a fracture or for dampness which might be caused by bleeding or incontinence. In this case, however, Jennifer was encased in a survival bag and maintaining what warmth she had was equally important, particularly with the blizzard raging round them. Stephen was able to check her head, neck, shoulders and chest. She had a bit of a gash on the side of her head just above her left ear but her skull seemed to be intact. The neck, shoulders and chest also seemed to be OK. However, just to be on the safe side, David dug out a cervical collar from the first aid kit and they put this on. Jennifer gave a groan while they were doing this and in the light of their head torches they could see that her eyes were open.

"Jennifer, I'm David from the tent next to you on the camp site. This is Stephen. Eric is also with us – you remember Eric from the pub last night?" There was no reply.

"You've had an accident and we need to check whether you have broken anything. Are you in pain anywhere? Do you feel sore?"

"Let's try her with some hot coffee," suggested Stephen rummaging around in his sack. "Here," he said, "try a sip of this. It will help to warm you up." He held her head and put the cup to her lips. The coffee spilled across her face and neck but she responded and some went in. He tried again, and a bit more went in this time. It seemed to revive her a bit.

"Jennifer, can you hear me?" asked David. She grunted.

"You've had an accident and we need to check if you have hurt yourself. Are you in pain anywhere? Are you sore?" he repeated.

"Cold," she said. " My leg," she added.

"Which leg?" asked David. "This one?" he said putting his hand on her left leg.

She flinched and nodded.

"Top or bottom?" he asked.

"Bottom."

"Anywhere else?" he asked

"Arm, I think," she said. "Numb."

"This one?" he asked, touching her left shoulder.

"Yes."

"OK, Jennifer, that's helpful. We are going to have to immobilise the injuries and then we will get you out of here," he said.

With some difficulty because of the bivouac bag, Stephen strapped the left arm across her chest with large triangular bandages. Meanwhile, David gently pulled her legs straight and strapped them together with triangular bandages tied tightly round the bivouac bag. Stephen gave Jennifer some more coffee and then David unpacked the warm air breathing apparatus from his sack and they got her to inhale some of this while they decided how best to get her down.

"Where's Stuart?" she asked.

It was the question David had been expecting but didn't really know how to answer. He thought it best to be honest. "I'm afraid he has been badly injured, but he is on his way to hospital in the helicopter," he said.

Tears welled up and then rolled down her cheeks but she didn't cry. David thought it best to leave her with her thoughts for a moment.

Stephen considered the options. "We are not going to be able to get one of our stretchers in here," he said. "The gully is too narrow. I think the best option is to put her into a chest and waist harness. We will get a third person up to guide her down the gully while we belay them. The third person can sledge her down the gully in her bivouac bag. The gully is relatively smooth and I think that will be easier than trying to get her onto someone's back in a carrying harness and taking her down piggy back. It's going to be uncomfortable but in these conditions speed is vital."

David radioed down to Alex to explain the position. Alex asked Paul and Ben to be ready to get the casualty onto the stretcher. Then he strapped on his crampons, tied onto the end of the spare rope David had taken up and he climbed up to a point just below the overhang while

David belayed him.

While this was going on, Stephen had explained the position to Jennifer. "I'm going to put you into a harness and then we are going to sledge you down to the bottom. Alex will be with you to guide you down while David and I lower you both. It will seem a bit precarious at first so you will have to help us and be brave. But we are all tied firmly to the cliff, so you will be quite safe – just a bit uncomfortable. Do you think you can do it?"

"Yes, I think so," she said after a moment.

"Good girl," said Stephen.

Stephen eased a climbing harness around Jennifer's waist and chest and tied his rope to it. In the meantime, David had taken up position to belay Alex with the rope attached to his harness. Alex clipped a belaying sling into his own harness and attached the other end to Jennifer's harness.

Now came the awkward part. David held Alex on a tight rope while Alex helped Stephen to manoeuvre Jennifer to the edge of the overhang. Jennifer gasped as she was lowered over the edge of the overhang seemingly into space. With some difficulty and at the cost of some pain to Jennifer, they got her over the edge and down into the continuation of the gully.

"You all right?" David called to Jennifer.

"You certainly win the prize for silly questions," she responded sharply. He took that as a good sign of recovery of spirit.

"OK, let's go," said Alex. Stephen and David paid out the ropes while Alex made his way cautiously backwards down the gully guiding Jennifer. Fortunately, the bed of the gully, although steep, was smooth with hard packed snow and ice and Jennifer in her plastic bivouac bag slid smoothly down.

Arriving at the bottom, willing hands disentangled them from their harnesses and Jennifer was lowered onto the casualty bag which was laid out on the stretcher. With difficulty because of the noise of the wind, Ben introduced himself to Jennifer and gave her a quick examination. Reasonably satisfied with what he saw, she was zipped into the warmth of the bag and strapped onto the stretcher. Eric managed to make himself known notwithstanding being muffled up to the eyeballs in his waterproofs. She was obviously pleased to have someone there she knew so he stayed by her. Paul informed Control via the relay that the casualty was down and that they were starting the carry. Then, as the wind had risen further still and the snow was once more blowing horizontally, the first carrying party took up the stretcher and started making their way from Angle Tarn up towards the top of Rossett Gill.

Alex waited at the bottom of the gully while David abseiled down in the teeth of the gale with Stephen belaying him.

"Happy New Year," shouted Alex as he joined him.

"So it is," said David and they shook hands.

Stephen meanwhile had sacrificed a belay sling and abseiled down to join them. They coiled up the ropes, packed up the gear, hoisted it onto their backs and, with heads down against the gale, followed the stretcher party towards Rossett Gill.

Lingcove Beck, midnight

Although he had felt guilty about leaving Sam, Adam had been pleased to be doing something positive after lying for so long in the ruined sheep fold. He had been surprised when he worked it out to discover that he had been there for about nine hours. He felt sure that the absence of any sign of rescue must mean that something had happened to Lucy. The fact that Sam and Lucy were now relying on him had given him a much needed spur.

What he had not counted on was feeling so weak. The relentless wind and snow, the wet, cold and general discomfort of the sheepfold and the constant worry over such a long period had all combined to sap his physical condition. Even with his head torch to light the way, it had been hard work wading through the snow and his progress from the beginning had been much slower than he had expected. He had not really thought about the sort of conditions that Lucy would have had to struggle with during the blizzard. It was just as well, he had thought as he set out, that conditions had eased. Fortunately, route finding was not a problem. Although he had been unable to see anything beyond the beam of his torch, he just had to head south west keeping the stream on his right.

The wind and the snow had caught him out about ten minutes after he had started. Several huge gusts signalled the return of the blizzard. The snow started again and then the over a period of a few minutes the wind built up to a steady gale. He thought about returning to the sheep fold but rejected the idea. The prospect of turning round and fighting his way back against the wind and the snow was not attractive; at the moment the wind was helping him along. Furthermore, he reminded himself, Sam and Lucy were now both relying on him so he had to go on. He zipped up his jacket as far as it would go, pulled the hood of his jacket as tight around his head as he could and pressed on.

Advanced base, 12.45am

At advanced base, Joe had just taken the message from Langdale Alex about the successful evacuation of the casualty from the gully when three young men came into the hut. Joe asked them to wait a moment while Bill Williams arranged for an ambulance to come out to the Old Dungeon Ghyll Hotel to collect Jennifer. He advised ambulance control in Kendal that the casualty would be unlikely to arrive at the ODG for a further two to three hours, probably nearer the latter. Ambulance control thought it might be sensible to allow an hour to get from Kendal to the ODG in present conditions and arranged for an ambulance to depart in an hour's time.

"Can we help you lads?" asked Joe when Bill had put down the phone.

"Well, it may be nothing," said the tallest of the three strangers. "Normally we would have left it until the morning, but we heard the helicopter earlier on and realised there must be a rescue going on, so we thought we would come and have a word with you. Me and my mate," he said pointing to the shorter lad beside him, "we're camping up at the National Trust camp site. There is a tent next to us and it's empty. We thought first of all that the people must be over at the Old Dungeon Ghyll seeing in the New Year; but the bar has closed now and no one has shown up."

"You were quite right to come and tell us," said Bill, "but I think we are ahead of you. We are already looking for the occupants of a tent at the camp site."

"Oh well, that's a relief," said the tall one again. "I'm sorry to have troubled you. Can I ask if they are they all right? We didn't really get to speak to them but they seemed a lively party."

"Well, I can't really tell you at this stage," said Bill. "One is on his way to hospital and the other is still being brought off the mountain."

The tall one and his mate looked at each other. "What about the other two?" asked the short one. There was silence.

"I think you had better start again," said Joe quietly. "What do you mean by 'party'?" he asked.

"There were two men and two women," said the short one, "all in their mid to late twenties I should think."

Bill and Joe looked at each other. "This sounds like a different group altogether," said Joe. "Come and sit down."

Five minutes later the pair, Roger and James, were on their way back to the camp site in the police Land Rover with Bill and Matthew.

The third one remained behind. "Was there something else?" asked Joe.

"Well, yes," he said, "there is. I'm from the press; I'm freelance." He produced his press card. "My name's Richard Hope. I'm a freelance journalist. I contribute a column to the local paper from time to time. You may have seen it. I was aware that a rescue was going on and I was over speaking to the other lads at the camp site. I wondered if I could sit in and just watch what happens. I doubt if many people know what is actually involved in a rescue and I think it would be of considerable interest."

Joe's immediate reaction was to ask him to leave; but he thought about it for a moment before concluding that his instinct was right. "No, I'm sorry," he said. "We will be having a casualty coming through soon and it looks as though there may be another rescue to organise. This is not a large hut and I'm afraid you would be in the way. I'm willing to consider the idea for a future occasion; but tonight could be difficult."

"Can you at least give me some information about the first rescue?" he asked.

"No, not until I have more details myself and not until we have notified relatives," said Joe incautiously. "There will be a press release later in the day."

"So, are you saying that there has been a fatality?" asked the journalist scribbling in his note book.

"No, I'm not," said Joe.

"Then why are you notifying relatives?"

"Look, I have things to do and I must ask you to leave please," said Joe with some impatience.

The response clearly disappointed the young man as he saw his scoop fading away. "It would be good publicity for you," he suggested.

"That doesn't worry me too much," said Joe shortly. His mind was already turning to the problems of dealing with a second rescue on a night like this.

"Well perhaps it should," said the journalist realising that he was getting nowhere. To Joe's relief, he picked up his jacket and left.

Meanwhile the police Land Rover had arrived at the camp site. Roger took Bill and Matthew to the tent which Peter and Adam had had such a struggle to put up last night.

"This is a different tent," said Matthew to Bill. "The one we have been involved with up till now is further over."

"Is there anything more we can do to help?" asked Roger.

"No, not unless there is anything further you can tell us about the group," replied Bill; "but thanks for alerting us. Which is your tent in case we need to have a further word with you?" James pointed to the two man tent nearby.

Roger and James disappeared into their tent. Bill unzipped the door to the big family tent and, with the aid of their torches, he and Matthew conducted a search. They were looking for identification, any indication of route planning and the number and make of their car. At the end of ten minutes they had established that the party comprised four people who had probably come up from London: Peter Stansfield, Adam Moore, Lucy Croft and one other. They had been unable to find any identification for Sam. There was no indication of route planning; but nor was there any walking gear in the tent. The absence of jackets, boots and rucksacks suggested that the group were probably wearing them wherever they were. The presence of fresh food indicated that the party intended to return to the tent in the near future; but whether they had planned to return tonight was not clear. Matthew found a set of car keys with a Volkswagen key ring among Peter's possessions.

Having finished with the tent for the time being, they zipped it up and made their way over to a Volkswagen estate parked near the tent. The key ring contained a remote control locking device. When Matthew tried it, there was a bleep and the lights flashed on the car as the doors unlocked. They cleared the snow from the car and, while doing so, Bill came across a very soggy note tucked under the windscreen wipers. An examination in the light of a torch showed that unfortunately the ink had run and the message was smudged and almost illegible. Bill put it carefully away. They searched the car but came up with no additional useful information other than Peter's address which was noted in the car documents. Bill and Matthew climbed into their Land Rover. They checked both hotels on the way back to the Advanced Base. The New Year celebrations were ended and the bars had closed. The weather had discouraged revellers from milling around outside and they had quickly dispersed into the night. Neither hotel had any record of a Peter Stansfield or of a group of four from London.

Back at Advanced Base, Bill and Matthew explained the position to Joe. Bill then got on the phone to the Rescue Co-ordination Centre at RAF Kinloss to thank them for their assistance in the rescue, to say that they now appeared to have another rescue on their hands, but that the weather had closed in again. In view of the conditions, said the Co-ordination Centre, the helicopter had been directed back to Bulmer once it had unloaded the casualty at Lancaster Hospital. When visibility eventually improved again, said Bill, further assistance from the chopper would be very welcome. The Co-ordination Centre promised to keep the position under review.

Lingcove Beck, 12.45am

Adam was regretting having given his jumper to Sam. The relentless wind seemed to find its way through his supposedly wind proof jacket and he was feeling very cold. He was shivering as he struggled along and, if he relaxed his mouth, his teeth started chattering. He had often heard the phrase 'teeth chattering' and was surprised how apt it was. He thought longingly of the warm fire, the cosy bar and the crowds enjoying the New Year celebration at the Old Dungeon Ghyll that they had been so looking forward to. It was all beginning to seem a bit unreal; indeed, he wondered if this was all a bad dream and he would wake up shortly in a comfortable bed to find all was well. At that moment, he lost his footing and crashed down into the snow. That certainly seemed real enough.

"Happy bloody New Year," he thought.

He struggled to his feet and went on. He shouted curses at the weather and that gave him some relief, so he spent a few minutes yelling every possible obscenity he could think of at the elements.

He couldn't hear the stream, nor could he see it; but then he couldn't hear anything but the wind, nor could he see anything but the snow in the limited beam of his torch. He thought he had better check his general direction with the compass but was shocked when he couldn't find it. He stopped and took off his gloves and tried every pocket in his jacket without success. With horror he realised it had probably dropped out of a pocket when he had fallen over. He wondered about retracing his steps but knew that the prospects of being able to find it in these conditions must be almost nil.

The answer was to move closer to the stream and follow that; it should be over to his right. He waded through the snow in that direction; but when he hadn't come upon it after about five minutes, he thought that, with the force of the wind, he had probably not turned sufficiently to his right - so he turned further. The wind and the snow were now coming straight at him and he still had enough sense to realise that that must be the wrong direction. Indeed, he thought, if he put the wind behind him, it would push him more or less in the right direction. So he turned round and tried to keep the wind behind him as he struggled on through the darkness and the snow.

It was not long before the going became harder and he realised that he must be going up hill. Without a map, he couldn't tell whether he should be; but the wind was still coming from behind so he persevered. What he had failed to take into account was that the wind was blowing him in a southerly direction while the stream was flowing south west. The longer he continued in his present direction, the further away from the stream he was getting.

Adam found it difficult to think clearly with the wind howling around him and visibility limited to the dim light of his head torch. After a while, he realised that he had been right the first time; the key to finding his way was, indeed, the stream. Unless he could find it, he was in trouble. Once he found it, he should keep it on his right side and just follow it and it would take him inevitably to the farm. Logic suggested that if he went downhill keeping the wind on his right side he must eventually come to the stream. So turning so as to put the wind on his right side, he went on into the darkness. At once the going became easier and he realised he was going downhill.

He didn't see the cliff in the light of his head torch; he just walked straight over the edge. Fortunately, it was only a short drop, some twenty feet or so, and he landed at the bottom almost before he realised he was falling and then tumbled on down the slope. The snow cushioned his landing but it was still severe enough to knock the breath from his body. Then his head connected with a boulder and he knew nothing else.

Rossett Gill, 1.15am

Carrying a stretcher down a mountain-side is a tiring business at the best of times. Carrying it in the dark, in the worst blizzard of the winter with the wind shrieking around their ears, after several hours ranging around the mountains in unpleasant conditions, is exhausting. While the stretcher is constructed to operate as a sledge, this is not possible over rough ground and certainly not possible down the top third of Rossett Gill. There was room for three carriers each side on the stretcher, each with a carrying strap to distribute the weight across the shoulders. Alex insisted on frequent change overs. A couple of team members scouted ahead to guide the stretcher bearers down the best route. Inevitably, there were slips. Mostly these involved a single carrier and the remaining bearers managed to cope; but on two occasions, the slip was more serious and involved all the carriers losing their footing and the stretcher ending up on the ground. Jennifer cried out on the first occasion; but on the second she bore it stoically. David thought she recognised just how much effort was required that night to get her off the mountain. She seemed to be conscious throughout the whole journey; but the howling of the wind made it impossible to talk and her face was covered over for much of the journey to protect her from the snow.

Advanced base, 1.00am

The report from Bill and Matthew on their visit to the camp site presented Joe with some difficult decisions. He discussed these with the other three. The first and in a way the easiest question was how to treat the information. As with the call out for Stuart and Jennifer, it was by no means certain that anyone was in difficulties. Indeed, given that it was

New Year's day it was quite possible that the party were still seeing in the New Year somewhere. On the other hand, the smudged note had not been removed from the car windscreen and all the bars in the vicinity were closed. Normal practice was to treat such cases as though there was a problem, so he had to work on the assumption that there was a party in difficulty.

The next and altogether more difficult question was how to respond. With the weather deteriorating again and wind force 10, gusting 11 - possibly 12, forecast for the tops, he didn't think he should be sending parties out to check the mountain tops. Had they not found Jennifer, he would have been withdrawing his teams from the hills now until conditions picked up again. As it was, there was no question of the helicopter returning until the weather improved so the Hanging Knotts casualty was having to be carried out; and a long and difficult carry it would certainly be. So he simply didn't have the manpower to divert to another search. He could always do a further trawl of absent team members to see whether any more were available. Although there were twenty on the hill at the moment, there were a further eight on the books who could be called again. He could also call out another rescue team as back up. That was the usual response to multiple call outs. But with the weather building up, he couldn't send them up onto the tops. So any search at this stage would have to be low level, simply checking the main paths up to the tops.

There was a further consideration. It was New Year's Eve. Many people would have been partying. Joe remembered there had been a call out one summer when several members of the team had been enjoying themselves alcoholically at a fancy dress barbecue. Fortunately, the call out was to a rescue rather that a search. Someone had fallen and broken a leg near Three Tarns. More than one member of the team had said afterwards that they had had no recollection of how they came to be up at Three Tarns. Fortunately also, it had been a sunny day and the alcoholic glow had worn off by the time they had arrived there. The casualty's reaction to being rescued by an assortment of chimney sweeps, rag and bone men and Roman soldiers is not recorded. But there could be no question on a night like this of calling out people who had been partying. So manpower could be a problem. He had been lucky with the first call out; he had caught people before they had left home.

That brought him to the last and most difficult question. Where to look for the party assuming he could raise the manpower? Try as they might, they had been unable to decipher the note on the car windscreen. The words had smudged so much that it was no longer possible to determine the number of words in the note, let alone what it said. Bill thought he could detect the words crag, tarn and pike in that order although whether they were in the singular or plural it was impossible to say. Joe was not so sure; but assuming Bill was correct, what did it tell them? Matthew suggested that the party may have intended to go up by Tarn Crag to Stickle Tarn and then on to the Langdale Pikes, all on the north side of the valley. Joe responded it could equally be a reference to Crinkle Crags and Three Tarns on the west side of the valley, although where pike came into that, he couldn't say. The only pikes on that side of the valley were Side Pike and Pike O'Blisco and they were in the other direction to the Three Tarns. Perhaps, said Bill, the tarn in question was Red Tarn in which case the party might be going by Crinkle Crags to Red Tarn and then up Pike O'Blisco.

With the recollection of the failure of his first search and rescue as team leader very much in mind, Joe was reluctant to commit himself without wringing the last drop of information from the note. With the aid of the map, they discussed every possible permutation for a while but inevitably just went round in circles. Joe cursed the writer of the note for not having the sense to put it in some form of plastic cover. In the end, however, he felt he was unable to make a decision on the basis of the note. All that could be said with certainty was that the party had walked from the camp site and, from what the two lads had said, they had not left until late morning. So that limited the area of search. As a working hypothesis, Joe could assume from the search already undertaken that they were nowhere on the main path from Rossett Gill, to the Ore Gap, over Bowfell, and down by the Three Tarns and the Band; nor were they along the climbers' traverse below Bowfell Buttress. Teams had also covered Hell Gill and most of the Crinkle Crags which left only the main track up Browney Gill and Pike O'Blisco to be searched on the west and south west side of the valley. The party might, of course, have strayed from the main path, in which case they could be anywhere in that area. There was not a lot he could do about that. A more extensive check would have to wait until the weather improved sufficiently to enable them to mount a sweep search. The initial focus of his manpower resources, thought Joe, should probably be on the north side of the

Langdale valley – Stickle Ghyll, Tarn Crag, Stickle Tarn, Pavey Ark, Harrison Stickle, Pike of Stickle and the Stake Pass. That fitted Matthew's interpretation of the note, although Joe was disinclined to attribute much weight to that.

Of course, the party might have got lost by Esk Hause and strayed into Borrowdale; they might have got lost on the Crinkles and have ended up near the Three Shires Stone or have headed off into Eskdale; or they might have got lost on the Langdale Pikes and ended up in Grasmere. The permutations were not exactly endless but they were certainly numerous. Joe remembered the call out some years earlier to look for a walker who had announced to the landlady of his bed and breakfast that he proposed to walk down Borrowdale with a view to climbing Helvellyn. As Borrowdale is not a means of direct access to Helvellyn, every team in the Lake District had been called out when he had eventually been reported overdue by the landlady. Curiously, the walker had eventually been found on Helvellyn but by that time he was dead.

Having determined on a course of action, Joe got on the phone to the absent team members. Of the eight, he eventually roused four. Two of them had been celebrating the New Year too much to be of any use. The other two, Tom and Tania, said they could come. Joe suggested that, in view of conditions, they might want to liaise over transport. Joe then phoned Moss Henderson, the team leader of the Glenridding Mountain Rescue Team. The Glenridding team normally act as back up for the Elterwater team for searches and multiple rescues. It is a reciprocal arrangement. Joe explained the position and asked him whether he thought he could get his team over Kirkstone Pass to Langdale given the snow. Moss said that, even if he could raise enough team members, he thought it would be difficult. Joe said he had better have a word with the South Lakeland Fell Rescue Team instead. As they were based in Kendal, getting to Langdale should be easier.

So Joe phoned John Patterson, the team leader, and got him out of bed. He again explained the position. They discussed what was possible in the conditions. Like Moss Henderson, John thought there might be manpower problems as a result of New Year celebrations but he would see what he could do. He agreed that a low level search of main paths made sense. He said it might be at least an hour and a half before he could get any of his team to the New Dungeon Ghyll Base. He would bring the first Land Rover as soon as it was full. The second could follow on later.

Joe thanked him and rang off.

Joe then phoned the team leaders of the Borrowdale and Ravenglass Mountain Rescue Teams. He couldn't get hold of the team leader of the Borrowdale team but he managed to get his deputy. Joe recounted the information received, explained that the main paths up Bowfell and Crinkle Crags had already been searched and that South Lakeland Fell Rescue Team would shortly be covering the main paths on the north side of the Langdale Valley. He went on to say that the party might have got lost in the poor conditions and have strayed over into Eskdale or Borrowdale. He asked whether they could be in a position to start a search of the obvious routes from Langdale into their areas at first light. Both said they would put that in hand.

Advanced base, 2.00am

Tania and Tom had liaised over transport as suggested. Tom had volunteered to take his car as he had had a quiet New Year celebration and had collected Tania on the way.

Tom had admired Tania from a distance for as long as he had known her – all of eighteen months. So far as he knew she was unattached; indeed, she exuded a sort of no nonsense approach which seemed designed to keep the male population at bay. Some men would also be uncomfortable about her physical equality. Like others, Tom found her a bit daunting and his shyness had inhibited him from taking the initiative.

Tom had been plagued by shyness for as long as he could remember. He thought it might have had something to do with being sent away to school at an early age. His father had been in the Foreign Office and he and his mother had spent many years abroad. He was an only child and being alone with complete strangers in an environment hidebound by tradition and discipline had forced him in upon himself. He had learned to contain his emotions and over time had necessarily become self-reliant, a characteristic which the school syllabus had reinforced with its emphasis on outdoor activities. The strong hierarchical organisation of the boarding school had given him an exaggerated respect for authority to the extent that, as a child, he had found it difficult to converse easily with adults and even now found himself uneasy speaking with superiors at work. His awkwardness meant that he had not made friends easily but when he had, they had endured. The boarding school had been single sex, so that Tom had had no experience of girls until he went to university. The egalitarian approach of university life had been both a shock and a release for him but one he had been slow to adjust to. His shyness had remained and he had come to dread the exposure to which he had been subjected in small group teaching on which the university unfortunately laid stress. His relationship with women had been awkward until he lost his virginity - almost by accident. He had come home one night to the flat he shared with a friend to find the friend away but his girlfriend installed by mistake in his (Tom's) bed. Far from rectifying the mistake, the girlfriend had obligingly made room for him. The experience had given him some much-needed confidence and in his final year at university he had begun to come out of himself. He still found himself uneasy in large groups and that was why his New Year celebrations had been muted.

Tom had been secretly delighted when Joe had suggested he liaise with Tania over transport. Tania for her part had seen in the New Year with some friends but had decided not to go on to a party and was tucked up in bed when the phone went. She was not best pleased at the prospect of a night on the hills, particularly a night like this. When Tom arrived she had climbed into the car and, apologising for her rudeness, had dozed off. Tom had concentrated on the driving and it had taken all his concentration. It was with considerable relief that he eventually turned into the New Dungeon Ghyll Hotel car park.

They collected their gear and went across to advanced base. The hut seemed like an oasis of heat and light in the cold and the dark of the snow storm.

Joe recounted what information they had on the missing group of four. He explained that, because the Elterwater team was already committed on the other rescue, he had called in the South Lakeland team to start a search of the main paths on the north side of the valley. He asked Tom and Tania if they would cover the main track up Browney Gill to Pike O'Blisco and Red Tarn, that being the only route which had not been covered on the west side of the valley. He would give them further instructions once they arrived at Red Tarn but, possibly, he would want them to continue across to the Three Shires Stone on Wrynose Pass. They would have to use their discretion as to how high they went; conditions were decidedly unpleasant and were expected to get worse. It would probably be wise to keep off the tops.

Tom and Tania collected a flashlight and went out into the night.

John Patterson was not far out in his estimate. It was almost 2.30am when the first Land Rover from the South Lakeland Fell Rescue Team pulled into the car park at the New Dungeon Ghyll Hotel.

Joe was pleased to see him and introduced him to the two policemen. John remarked that the conditions on the roads were very unpleasant. Bill said that, in view of the volume of traffic likely to be involved in both rescues, it would be as well to get the local authority to divert a snow plough to clear the road down the Langdale valley as a matter of priority. He phoned the Roads Department emergency number and put that in hand.

Joe outlined to John Patterson the current position on the first rescue. He then explained what he knew about the party of four and went on to say why he felt the sensible option was to concentrate resources on the north side of the valley. He mentioned that Langdale Tania was covering the route to Red Tarn.

They discussed the routes to be covered. John had squeezed nine team members with him into the first Land Rover. A further five would be coming in the second. Joe suggested dividing the first party in three and sending one group up Stickle Ghyll to Stickle Tarn and the second and third groups up Dungeon Ghyll to cover the paths via Pike How to Harrison Stickle and via Thorn Crag to Pike O'Stickle. The group in the second Land Rover could check the route to Pike O'Stickle via the Stake Pass at the end of Mickleden.

Joe then outlined the position so far for the benefit of the South Lakeland team members and went through the geography of the search area and how it was to be covered at this stage by reference to the large scale map on the wall. He stressed that weather conditions were very unpleasant and forecast to get worse and that leaders of the individual search groups must consider the safety of team members as their first priority. It would not help anyone, least of all the missing group, if resources had to be diverted to extracting team members who had pushed themselves too far in these conditions. They should keep off the tops and not be shy of going to ground or withdrawing if conditions got too bad.

John then divided his team members into three groups of three and allocated tasks and call signs to them. Bill Williamson made a careful note of who was with which group. Then the three groups set off. John stayed to help Joe at Control.

Ambulance headquarters, Kendal, 1.45am

At 1.45 am ambulance control had asked two of the paramedics on standby, Jim and Angela, to respond to the request from the police for an ambulance to go to the Old Dungeon Ghyll Hotel. The two had been happy to do so; it would be a change from tending to New Year revellers. The controller passed on such information as he had been given about the nature of Jennifer's injuries and told them to be careful once they got off the main A591 road at Ambleside. It had been snowing hard and it was probable that the snow ploughs had not yet cleared the minor roads.

Angela had not realised until they drove out of the station that it had started snowing again. She was not particularly worried; the main road from Kendal to Ambleside had, indeed, been cleared although she noted that the new snow was beginning to settle. She drove carefully, aware that there was no rush. The casualty was being carried down and would not arrive at the Advanced Base, it was thought, for another hour at least, probably more.

Ambleside was surprisingly quiet at this early hour for New Year's Eve. Probably the revellers were all indoors. It was snowing hard and the wind was blowing the snow almost horizontal. The wipers on the ambulance were working hard to keep the windscreen clear. The street lights and the Christmas lights suspended across some of the streets helped to give her a reference but she began to realise that conditions would be unpleasant once they got into the Langdale valley. She wondered what conditions were like up in the mountains and was glad the casualty was being brought to them rather than the other way round.

They crossed Brathay Bridge and drove out through Clappersgate. Once they were beyond the street lighting, their speed dropped considerably. She found it was best to keep the headlights dipped, but even so visibility was severely limited by the driving snow. The wipers seemed to be fighting a losing battle to keep the snow from piling up on the windscreen. Her field of vision was restricted to a square in the middle of the screen as the snow worked its way in from the edges. This must be a bit like driving a tank she thought with the driver peering through a sort of letter box. The snow on the road was also much deeper now. There had been traffic this way recently and she followed the tram lines left in the snow as far as Skelwith Bridge. When she turned off by the Inn, the tram lines in the snow turned with her. They had been left by Tom's car and by the South Lakeland Fell Rescue Team Land Rovers which had passed this way shortly before. Jim had been on the radio to the station to let them know of the conditions but there was not much that headquarters could do beyond urging caution.

Angela found she was tensing up over the wheel, hardly surprising in the circumstances she thought. She tried to relax and drove with an eye fixed on the bottom of the nearside dry stone wall for want of any other reference. She became mesmerised by the glare from the headlights reflecting off the snow and the ambulance veered into the side and there was an awful noise as it scraped along the verge and glanced off the wall. Angela swung the wheel and the vehicle skidded slightly as it regained the middle of the road.

"Sorry," she said. "It's a bit difficult seeing where we are going."

"That's OK," said Jim. "You are doing fine. We are in no hurry so just take you're time."

They emerged onto Elterwater Common and left the dry stone walls behind. Angela was at first relieved. However, she quickly realised that she now had no reference whatsoever and she could no longer distinguish the road from the surrounding countryside. The tram lines in the snow from previous vehicles had been more or less covered over so she slowed right down and Jim wound down his window and leaned out to see if he could guide her. They could do with snow poles such as she had seen in places in Scotland she thought. Twice in the next five minutes as she crept across the common the ambulance lurched as it mounted the verge; both times she managed to get it back onto the road before it got bogged down. Then they were across and driving through the village of Chapel Stile. The walls had returned to define the side of the road for her and she could relax a bit.

"You couldn't see if you could clear some of the snow of the windscreen could you?" she asked Jim.

Jim unclipped his seat belt and leaning out he reached round and across the windscreen and scraped as much of the snow off as he could. Some of it managed to work its way up his sleeve to his discomfort.

"That's better," said Angela.

They continued slowly on along the valley with Jim occasionally reaching out to try and clear the snow off the windscreen. Angela maintained a reasonable speed to ensure they did not get bogged down in the snow. She was less tense now and had a better feel for the handling of the vehicle in these conditions.

It all happened very quickly. The offside wall loomed large in her headlights as they entered a sharp left hand just beyond the farm house at Robinson Place. Angela was was not aware she was into a bend until too late. It caught her by surprise and she instinctively braked hard. The ambulance skidded in the snow and she lost control. It slewed sideways and then rammed into the wall. Jim, who had not clipped back into his seat belt, went through the windscreen. Angela just had time to register surprise at the force of the impact before her head came into contact with the upright stanchion of the offside door frame and she knocked herself out. As sometimes happens in an accident, the horn jammed itself on and announced to an empty world that there was a vehicle at the bend in the road.

Advanced base, 3.45am

Rossett Gill seemed to be much longer than David remembered it; or perhaps it was just that tonight he was counting every step. But eventually it ran out into the flatter ground of the Mickleden valley. Alex gave them a five minute break and Ben checked Jennifer's condition. He seemed reasonably satisfied. Then it was off down the two miles of snow covered valley. To their relief, they had been able to sledge the stretcher down much of the made up section of the track down Rossett Gill and they were able to sledge it much of the way along Mickleden. The stretcher was fitted with skis for winter use. It was clear, however, that even fairly slight bumps were uncomfortable for Jennifer and from time to time they had to carry it while wading through deep snow.

At length, after a carry from Angle Tarn lasting almost three hours, the buildings of the Old Dungeon Ghyll Hotel appeared through the driving snow. Joe and Matthew had brought the team Land Rovers round but there was still no sign of the ambulance. The stretcher was loaded into the back of one of the vehicles. Ben and Eric climbed into the back to keep an eye on Jennifer while the rest of the team distributed themselves around the remaining seats for the short trip to the advanced base. Those without seats walked the additional half mile.

When the casualty arrived at advanced base, Bill got onto the ambulance control and explained that the ambulance had still not shown up. The control said they had heard nothing either which suggested that it had got into difficulty somewhere. Joe said he couldn't wait any longer. He would arrange for one of the team Land Rovers to get the stretcher on its way to Kendal. They should meet the ambulance on the way and could decide whether to transfer the stretcher at that stage.

David volunteered Eric and himself to take the Land Rover as they had both met Jennifer and Joe agreed. Ben said he would come along too just to see her safely to hospital. Joe asked David to hang on for a moment and then introduced John Patterson to the assembled team members. He was already known to many of them; those involved in mountain rescue in the Lake District were a fairly small community. Joe went on to explain that another group might be missing and that a second search was getting under way. He outlined what Bill and Matthew had found at the camp site. In view of the weather, the search would initially be confined to low level paths on the Langdale Pikes side of the valley for the time being and was being carried out by the South Lakeland Fell Rescue Team. Tania and Tom, meanwhile, were checking out the path to Red Tarn which had not been covered in the first search.

He suggested that those team members who had been out on the hills all night should help themselves to the soup and sandwiches that Bill had managed to lay on with the willing co-operation of the hotel. Then they should take themselves off back home using whatever vehicles were available and get a few hours sleep and some food. Unless they were lucky, it looked as though they would be required again as soon as the weather eased a little. He suggested that team members meet at the Elterwater base at 2pm and that further instructions would be given at that time. If the party was found before then he would notify them.

"Oh yes, Happy New Year," he said. "I'm sorry you have not been able to celebrate it." There was a chorus of greetings in response and a general round of hand shaking. Then team members moved off to get a bite to eat before heading for home.

No one paid much attention to a stranger who was also nibbling at a sandwich and passing from group to group. After leaving the Advanced Base, Richard Hope had decided to wait until the casualty was brought down in the hope of being able to catch one or two team members in an unguarded moment. His journalistic experience suggested that, while people were uncommunicative during an event, they tended to unwind afterwards. He would be surprised if he did not find out much of what had happened. The laying on of soup and sandwiches had been a bonus. It provided a forum for the unwinding process and he managed to gate crash without being noticed. To those who asked, he passed himself off as a friend of the missing couple from the camp site and gave the impression that he had been involved in some way with the search. His boldness paid off. Team members, not surprisingly, were discussing the events on the hill and, with the occasional question, he was eventually able to assemble an outline of what had happened. What particularly interested him was the second search that was in progress and he queried how on earth anyone knew where to start looking. Greg Meecham obliged him by saying that this was down to the team leader and that Joe was pretty experienced now, although he had had to learn the hard way. The journalist was then treated to a synopsis of Joe's first search and rescue as team leader.

Meanwhile, the first Land Rover was on its way to Kendal Hospital with Jennifer. David had explained the position to Jennifer and had apologised for what would be a bit of a bumpy ride. She was pleased to be in the warmth of the vehicle and had shown signs of going to sleep. Eric and Ben had climbed into the back with the stretcher and Stephen and Shelagh had taken the two spare seats at the front as far as Elterwater. David had slipped the vehicle into gear and they had set off down the road.

It was snowing heavily and visibility with dipped headlights was limited to a few metres. David drove in the middle of the road and kept one eye on the dry stone walls on either side. Everyone was very tired.

As they came round the bend at Robinson Place they saw why the ambulance had not arrived. It was slewed across the road blocking it with its front offside embedded in the wall. The passenger was visible having apparently gone through the windscreen. There was no sign of the driver who was presumably still inside. It was turning into a very long night.

Shelagh got on the radio to advanced base while Ben and Eric got out and went over to examine the passenger. Stephen and David went round to see what had happened to the driver. They had some difficulty forcing open the door as it had buckled. The driver, a young woman, was clearly alive because she was groaning. She was still strapped into her seat but a quick examination with a flashlight showed a nasty bruise with some broken skin on her temple where she seemed to have come in contact with the door frame.

"Hello," said Stephen to the driver, "can you hear me? My name is Stephen."

He was rewarded with a groan. "You have had an accident so just sit still while we have a look at you. Can you tell me your name?"

The driver mumbled something and Stephen bent down to hear. "Sorry, I didn't catch that," he said.

The driver mumbled again.

"Did you say Angela?" asked Stephen.

There was a nod.

"OK, Angela, you seem to have a gash on your head where you bent the door. The door seems to be beyond repair but your head doesn't seem so bad." Stephen gently probed around it and the driver winced.

"Sorry," said Stephen. The skull seemed to be intact. "Do you have pain anywhere else?"

Angela thought vaguely that that was usually her line. It was curious to be on the receiving end of the question. "I don't think so," she said hesitantly.

Stephen gently went through an examination feeling for abnormalities and asking the driver whether she felt any pain.

"You seem to be OK, apart from the bruise on your head," said Stephen eventually. "We'll put a bandage on that. Do you want to come into the back of the ambulance and just rest for a bit with a blanket." Stephen helped Angela out of the driver's seat and round to the back where she settled her on one of the stretchers. David found some sterile wipes and cleaned up the gash and then put on a dressing.

Eric meanwhile, on Ben's instructions, was looking in the back of the ambulance for the first aid kit. The passenger was in a poor condition. He was unconscious but breathing and there was a pulse. Ben thought the neck might be broken, presumably the result of crashing through the windscreen. There were facial injuries but he did not think these were serious. The passenger was also very cold having been sprawled half out of the ambulance for sometime and Ben was worried about the effects of hypothermia.

"I'm going to immobilise the top half of his body," said Ben. "Then I think we should get him onto one of the stretchers in the ambulance while he warms up." It took a while to immobilise the passenger to Ben's satisfaction. Then they were able to lift him carefully through the wreckage of the windscreen and load him onto one of the ambulance stretchers.

Meantime, the second team Land Rover had arrived along with Matthew in the police Land Rover with blue lights going. Shelagh's call had brought the soup and sandwich session to a premature conclusion. Paul had followed in his car with several team members and Martin had brought Ben's car with a view to leaving it for him in Ambleside. The journalist had been able to offer a lift to two of the team members and was there also. All in all, there was quite a crowd assembled.

Alex suggested that the ambulance should be moved so that the Land Rover with Jennifer could get through. It could also take Angela to hospital for a check up at the same time. Ben said that the injured passenger should wait for another ambulance. The jolting of a Land Rover would do his injuries no good at all.

Moving the ambulance was easier said than done. The front offside wheel had buckled when it hit the wall. With some difficulty, it was manoeuvred away from the wall and parked at the side of the road just out of the bend. Matthew placed warning signs on the road in both directions. David helped Angela out of the ambulance and into the front of the Land Rover and wrapped a blanket around her. Stephen sat beside her while Eric and Shelagh got in the back beside Jennifer. Ben remained with the passenger. Then they got under way again.

At Elterwater, Stephen climbed out. Shelagh said she would accompany David with the casualties to hospital and she came round to the front to sit beside Angela. Eric remained with Jennifer who was complaining of feeling car sick. There was not much Eric could do except chat to her to try and get her mind off it. In the meantime, the only receptacle he could find in case she was sick was a climbing helmet. He kept this handy.

Browney Gill, 3.45am

Tom and Tania had plodded along Oxendale Beck following the same track that Langdale Greg had taken some hours before. They diverged from the track at the junction with Crinkle Gill and turned south crossing the footbridge and heading up Browney Gill towards Red Tarn. Their head torches had limited visibility in the driving snow but what they could see showed the hillside rising steeply ahead of them. However, the strong wind behind them helped them on their way and they were able to maintain a slow but steady pace. Tom carried the flashlight and every so often shone it around. As they climbed, so the wind strengthened and it was not long before they were being bowled along by the gale.

Telephone box, Eskdale, 3.45am

Lucy came too with a start. It was pitch dark and it took her a moment to work out where she was. Her head torch had given out and she couldn't see the face of her watch but guessed she must have been asleep for some hours. When she had discovered that the phone had been vandalised, she had collapsed onto the floor of the phone box in despair. She had had the sense to get herself into her survival bag but had then just given way to overwhelming tiredness. The phone box was cramped and Lucy was very stiff from sleeping in a hunched up position. Her ankle throbbed and her knees were sore. From where she was she could hear that the gale had blown up again.

She wondered what she should do. She could stay where she was and hope that someone would eventually come by. The phone box was not comfortable but at least it was shelter and she had some food and could suck the snow for water. She thought she could survive. But in these conditions, someone might not pass by for days. In the meantime, Peter, Adam and Sam would die. If she was honest with herself, Peter was probably already dead by now. Adam and Sam were still depending on her so she couldn't just do nothing. She knew that the village of Boot lay further down Eskdale but from what she could remember it was at least a couple of miles away and she did not think she had the strength to crawl that distance.

The vision of Brotherilkeld Farm, dark, closed and empty returned to her. She remembered that she had thought about breaking in. The more she thought about it the more she knew that that was what she would have to do. She would break in and use the phone. She might also find food and drink and a bed. She realised that she should have done that before rather than coming on to the phone box. Had she done so, Adam and Sam might already have been rescued. She felt she had made a real mess of things. Well, hindsight was a wonderful thing. She had enough sense to realise that there was nothing she could do about the past and there was no point in dwelling on it; she suspected she would have plenty of time for that later. She could still, however, try and do something about the future but the sooner she got on with it the better.

Having settled that, she struggled out of her survival bag and, stuffing it into her rucksack, she got up onto her good foot and pushed against the door of the phone box. It wouldn't open. After a moments reflection she realised that the snow must be piled up against it. Rage boiled up inside. She seemed to have been thwarted at every turn in trying to go for help. With a strength she did not know she had, she shoved hard at the door with her good foot braced against the other side of the phone box. She pushed and pushed and the door gave bit by bit until there was enough of a gap to squeeze through.

It was snowing hard and the wind was funnelling down the valley. She couldn't bring herself to go down on her knees and crawl. The farm track was level and although it was covered in snow she thought she could hop the few hundred yards back to the farm house. Setting her face to the gale she set off down the track taking it in easy stages. It took her about twenty minutes to make it to the front door again. There was a sash and case window to the side of the door. Lucy unstrapped her ice axe and smashed one of the panes. She then put her hand inside and undid the catch and with some difficulty opened the window. She half expected to trigger a burglar alarm but then realised that that would be good as it might bring someone to investigate what was happening. In fact there was no alarm; she was surprised how straightforward it all was. She scrambled over the window ledge into a room. She took off her rucksack and began to feel along the wall until she came to the door. The light switch was beside the door. She took a deep breathe and depressed the switch – and there was light.

It looked as though she had broken in through the dining room window. She made her way into the hall and found the light switch by the front door. The phone was on the table in the hall. For a moment she was frightened to pick up the receiver. With all that had gone wrong till now, she fully expected to find that the telephone wasn't working because the line had come down in the gale.

However, when she eventually picked it up there was a reassuring dialling tone. She dialled 999.

Advanced Base, 4.15am

"Damn!" said Joe. "We've got everyone in the wrong place."

He had just put down the phone having received a call from the police conveying Lucy's message about the party in Eskdale. Lucy's message had been sufficiently comprehensive to make it clear that this was the party they were looking for. Visions of the first search he had organised as team leader when he had had all his resources on the wrong mountain flooded into his mind again. He stood there for a moment with a sense of hopelessness. Then he pulled himself together and got on the phone again to Miles Dawson, the team leader of the Ravenglass Mountain Rescue Team. The police had already alerted him.

Miles was, in some ways, the antithesis of Joe. He was assertive and decisive, very much the leader. This reflected his background. He had been brought up in Scotland and had been taught to ski almost as soon as he could walk. He had never taken to climbing but did a lot of mountain walking in his teenage years. He left school to join the army and was eventually commissioned into the parachute regiment. For the next ten years he enjoyed peacetime soldiering and the army encouraged his interests. He was sent to the Alps every year to take part in the inter-services ski championships where he skied for his regiment and for the army; he twice skied the Haute Route, the high level ski mountaineering route in the Alps, with an inter-services party; and every other summer, he joined a services expedition to explore some mountainous area of the world. In between he attended endless courses designed to make him competent to participate in, and subsequently to instruct in, a range of outdoor pursuits. He was never a climber in the sense that he climbed rock and snow and ice routes. He found he did not have that sort of head for heights. But he became an experienced mountaineer and was much in demand for expeditions as a good organiser.

His career in the army came to an abrupt end when an accident with a hand grenade left him with a severely damaged left hand. Miles found himself with a disability pension but no job in his early thirties. The prospect of a desk job did not interest him and he turned his attention to outdoor activity centres. After a couple of temporary posts as an instructor, he secured the position of director of an outward bound school. He had joined the Ravenglass Rescue Team and, in due course, was asked to take over as leader. Miles had no reservations about taking on the position. His military training had accustomed him to identifying an objective and allocating human resources to achieving it. He ran the team on more hierarchical lines than the Elterwater team but this was more a matter of emphasis than structure. Participation in decision-making was not exactly frowned upon in the Ravenglass team but it was not exactly encouraged either.

Joe explained to Miles what had been happening as regards the rescue at the Langdale end. He said he had two reasonably fresh team members up near Red Tarn, call sign Langdale Tania. If it would help, he would see whether they might be able to cut across and come down into the head of Eskdale via Swinsty Gill. Miles thought for a moment and then said he would appreciate any help he could get but not to put them at risk. It would take him at least an hour to get any of his team up to Brotherilkeld Farm, considerably longer if it was necessary to get a plough to clear the road first. It was then a long way up the valley to where the party seemed to have gone to ground. If there was a chance that Joe's people could get there first, that would be great.

Joe discussed the position with John Patterson and the two policemen. Tom and Tania were both fresh, experienced, fit and well-equipped. However, the weather on the hills was the worst it had been this winter and an obsession with safety was still ingrained in Joe. Nonetheless, their route if they crossed over to Eskdale would take them over a shoulder rather than up to a summit. Even so, it was not something to be embarked on lightly. The deciding factor was that the location of the casualties was known and there was a very good chance that Tania and Tom would be the first to get to them – and the sooner the better.

Joe got on the radio to Tom and Tania. "Langdale Tania, Langdale Tania, do you read me over?"

The crackling of the radio jerked Tom and Tania out of their reverie. The gale had prevented easy communication and they had each been buried in their own thoughts as they plodded steadily on up towards Red Tarn. Tom had been leading with Tania following close behind in his footsteps. Reception was poor; Tom could not even be sure of the sender or the intended recipient.

"Unidentified station, this is Langdale Tania," said Tom. "Unidentified station this is Langdale Tania. Reading you strength 2. Reading you strength 2. Over."

There was an unintelligible response.

"It's the gale," shouted Tania.

"It could be that Pike O'Blisco is blocking us," said Tom. He got out his mobile but then realised he didn't have the telephone number of advanced base; nor could he get any signal when he tried Donald at Elterwater headquarters.

"Let's move up the hill to the west and see if we can re-establish contact", shouted Tom. They turned and headed up towards Great Knott. Fifteen minutes later they stopped and tried the radio again. This time they managed a rather crackly exchange with Joe but they got the essence of the message. Joe emphasised that if conditions became too bad they should withdraw. He would remain on standby in case they needed to get in touch. Although conditions were bad, Tom and Tania thought they should be able to find their way across to Eskdale. Tom checked their position with the GPS. Tania took a bearing from the map to a point behind Crinkle Crags and above Swinsty Gill and Tom programmed the grid reference of their destination into his GPS. Then they set off in a north westerly direction with the wind now hindering rather than helping progress. They had emerged from the comparative shelter of Browney Gill and at around 2,000 feet they were experiencing the full force of the gale. They reckoned they had about a mile to go before they could begin their descent into Eskdale and their exposure to the wind and snow would increase as they continued upwards to about 2,500 feet. It was hard work pushing constantly against the wind but they were both fit and Tania thought they would be OK if conditions didn't get worse. If the worst came to the worst, they could always turn round and let the gale blow them across to the Three Shires Stone. What they would do then she hadn't thought.

The worst didn't come to the worst for about half an hour. Then quite unexpectedly the wind seemed to shift up a gear. It felt as though they had been physically hit by something. As the wind shrieked at them, Tom was sent staggering backwards while Tania was literally blown off her feet and sent bowling across the snow. Tom managed to tackle her before she had gone very far and they lay there together on the ground while the storm raged around them in the darkness.

"We passed some rocks about five minutes ago," yelled Tom. "They should give us some shelter. Do you think you can take us to them on a back bearing?" Meanwhile, he set the GPS for retracing his steps. Tania reversed the bearing on her compass. Then with an arm around each other to provide support in the wind they staggered back the way they had come.

What had taken them five minutes into the wind seemed to take no time at all with the wind helping them along. The rocks appeared almost immediately in the light of their head torches. They were no more than five or six feet high but, mercifully, one of them offered some sort of shelter on its leeward side.

"Ice axes," yelled Tom and together they frantically dug into the snow at the base of the rock to provide better shelter. The snow was not deep enough for digging a snow hole but after about ten minutes they had created a sort of trench large enough for them to get into. Tania got out her bivouac bag and they wrapped it around themselves and then rolled into the trench. The wind meantime continued to shriek across the plateau at hurricane force.

Tom and Tania were quiet for a moment lying with their arms wrapped around each other recovering their breath. Despite the shelter, the wind was savaging the bivouac bag.

"OK," said Tom eventually, "let's cheer ourselves up." With some difficulty, he managed to disengage himself from his rucksack and dug out the flashlight. He switched it on and the light against the bright colours of the bivouac bag lifted their spirits a bit. Then he got out his own bivouac bag and with some difficulty spread it underneath them to provide insulation.

"How about some coffee?" he said unscrewing the top of his flask and pouring a cup. Tania took a sip and felt the hot, sweet liquid coursing through her.

"Mmm, that's good," she said.

"Happy New Year," said Tom.

"Happy New Year," responded Tania with a grin and kissed him.

Tom's heart did a somersault. Tania took off her own rucksack and rummaged around until she found some chocolate and divided it between them.

"I think we are stuck here until the wind eases back to mere gale," she said.

"It might be as well if we radio in and let Control know," suggested Tom. Tania tried with her radio but could make no contact and Tom had no better success with his mobile.

"I could try sending a text message," said Tom, "but I can't send it to Joe or to Elterwater headquarters because I don't know their mobile numbers. In fact, come to think of it, I don't know the mobile number of anyone in the team."

"Well, whose number do you know?" asked Tania. "Bear in mind that it needs to be someone who is likely to have their phone beside their bed at this time of night."

Tom flicked through the numbers in his directory and then sent a short text message to a friend in Kendal simply asking him to acknowledge the message as a matter of urgency. He tried the same with two other numbers and then sat back and waited. His friend in Kendal had left his mobile in the kitchen so did not hear the message arrive. The owner of the second number had let the battery in his phone run down so he did not receive the message. The third number was his Mum's in Leeds. She had her mobile beside her bed. The persistent message signal woke her from a deep sleep.

"Yes," she said sleepily. Then she realised it was a text message and switched over. Having read Tom's message, she sent a short acknowledgement.

Tom was delighted when his message signal sounded. With some ingenuity, he crafted a short but explicit message to be phoned through to Control by his Mum saying that they had had to go to ground until the wind eased a bit. They were OK and would continue as soon as they could. About ten minutes later his Mum sent a text message back to say that Control had acknowledged. She told him to take care.

Tania was impressed. She had not yet mastered the use of text messaging and a vision of her Mum sending text messages in the middle of the night simply defied belief.

"We will need to watch we don't suffocate from new snow," said Tania. "We can probably let it go for half an hour then we had better check. In the meantime, let's get as comfortable as we can and try and keep warm." Tania laid out her rucksack as a sort of pillow and then they lay close together arm in arm. Outside, the wind continued to rage.

Tom had often fantasised about being arm in arm with Tania but never in his most optimistic moments did he ever think it would happen. Yet here he was. Admittedly it was not quite the situation he had visualised. Surprisingly, he felt relaxed and confident. Normally, he was found himself shy, tongue-tied and abrupt when talking to a girl.

"All I can say is that I am glad you are not Greg," said Tom. "I can't imagine feeling quite so good about lying close together arm in arm with him."

"Neither can I," responded Tania smilingly; then after a moment: "Are you really feeling good?"

"Yes," said Tom. "I don't feel good about the weather and about being stuck here when there are people in trouble. But if it has to be, well I would be hard put to think of someone I would rather be with."

Tania was silent. She had not really had occasion to think much about Tom until now. She was aware of him as a team member. She had categorised him as young, fit, reasonably good looking, undeniably competent, not 'one of the lads' and a bit awkward. Now she began to wonder whether the last part might just be due to shyness and a lack of confidence. In the short time they had been together, she had been impressed by his decisiveness when occasion required it. He had recognised the communication problem when they were in Browney Gill and acted to resolve it; he had taken the lead in going to ground when the hurricane force winds struck – she had been bowled over by the wind and might still be lying in the snow but for him; and he had seen a way of communicating with Control when she had assumed they had lost contact.

She was sensible enough to realise, however, that if she encouraged him, it might be difficult to disengage. He was a person who seemed to wear his heart very much on his sleeve. She valued her independence; she always had. It was probably the result of her upbringing.

Her father was a sheep farmer in Westmorland and she had grown up in the hills and from an early age had been accustomed to walking quite long distances whether to school or when working on the farm. Life on the farm had toughened her. She had learned to look after herself and to help around the house and on the farm. In contrast to Tom, her parents had brought her up to feel she was an equal and she was expected to behave as such. Like Tom, circumstances had made her self-reliant but, unlike Tom, she had gained in confidence as she grew and was at ease with adults – perhaps more so than with her peers. She had avoided many of the distractions and temptations to which teenagers are exposed, not from choice but for reasons of geography. Getting into town from the hill farm was something of an expedition that required pre-planning. Inevitably, she had missed out on things which others might regard as an important part of education for life; but she had made up for that through reading; she had become a voracious reader and a regular visitor to the travelling library. She had gone on from school to teacher training college to study physical education. College had been her first experience of life away from home; it was also her first experience of living in close association with men. She had been surprised by, and unaccustomed to, the shallow and superficial nature of much of the social life. It seemed to be a macho existence which centred on drinking, football, cars and sex. She had no objection to, but little interest in, drinking or football. Life on the farm had equipped her with a detailed knowledge of the anatomy of the internal combustion engine but no more than a limited knowledge of the anatomy of the human body. She quickly found, however, that there was no shortage of men keen to assist in this part of her education. She was not averse to experimentation and over the two years of her course she had the occasional affair. They had not lasted. She found that most of the men she went out with would see her as competition and as something of a challenge. They set out either to impress her or to show her that they were better than she was. They seemed not to value her for what she was. She had yet to meet someone she felt relaxed with; but then she had not really been looking.

If she was right about Tom's shyness, a relationship might help to relax him and bring him out a bit; and she did not think he would see her as competition.

"Are you offended?" asked Tom anxiously.

"No, not at all," she said, "just surprised;" and she kissed him lightly on the lips.

Tom's heart did several evolutions. When he had recovered he said:

"You know, I was always a bit frightened of you."

"You mean you no longer are? That's dreadful," she said teasingly. "What was frightening about me?"

"Well it's not easy to explain. It's this aura you convey. It's partly confidence and self-possession. It's partly the way you look directly at someone when you speak to them - well directly *up* at them to be more correct," he said with a reference to her five feet five inches. She jabbed him in the ribs. "And it's partly the way you speak your mind. All in all very daunting – a bit ice-maidenish!" he concluded.

"I'm not sure that is altogether a flattering picture," said Tania.

"Oh well, I omitted to mention that you look pretty good for your age. I can't speak for your figure because it is usually encased in windproof jacket and waterproof trousers; but the way your pony tail bounces around really turns me on." He reached up and removed her woollen hat and pulled out her pony tail. Then he ran his fingers gently through her hair and down her cheek.

Tania was startled by the speed at which things had developed and began to feel she was losing control of the situation. Her first thought was that she should stop this going any further; but she didn't. The complete unreality of their position was partly to blame. It had a liberating effect. With the storm raging all around them, she wanted to defy the elements; and rather to her surprise she found herself responding. With a sense of mischievousness she put her hand up to his face and gently kissed his chin, then his cheek and then his lips. As her lips parted, it was Tom's turn to be startled and his heart turned several more somersaults. The kiss was gentle, lasting and overpowering. It aroused them both and Tom's hand slid under her jacket and fleece to her woollen shirt. Taking his time, Tom slowly undid the buttons on her shirt and slipped his hand inside and round her back and hugged her to him.

"Hmm, that feels good," murmured Tania and they lay for a moment enjoying the intimacy while Tom stroked her back.

Then he reached up to unclip her bra and his hand moved round to cup one of her breasts and Tania gasped as his fingers gently caressed the firm nipple. They kissed again, long and lingeringly.

"I shall die from hypothermia," murmured Tania in his ear.

"Nonsense," said Tom, "lots of bodily warmth is just what the doctor ordered."

Over the next half an hour, while the storm raged on around them, their refuge provided an oasis of delight such as neither had experienced before. The tumult outside provided the back cloth for an encounter that was gentle and tender, unhurried and companionable, at times uncomfortable and cold, but most of all overwhelming. It took them away for a while from the precariousness of their position, away from the discomfort of their trench, from the clamour of the storm and from the frantic thrashing of the bivouac bag which threatened to tear itself apart. Against all the odds they found a moment of warmth and of peace.

Kendal Hospital, 5.15am

Conditions were difficult driving out of the Langdale Valley until they met the snow plough coming from the direction of Ambleside. After that things were relatively straightforward, except when they had to stop twice while Jennifer was sick into a climbing helmet. David made a careful note of which one it was for future reference. There was nothing they could do about the solid suspension and the bumpy ride through the snow didn't help. The snow seemed to ease a bit as they headed towards Windermere.

They were expected at Kendal Hospital and Jennifer was loaded onto a trolley and wheeled off for examination. Eric went with her so that she would have a face she knew. Angela was known to the staff and was surrounded by friendly faces. Indeed, the sympathy was all too much for her. She had been feeling tearful during the drive, reproaching herself for the injury to Jim. Shelagh had tried to reassure her. Now she burst into tears. She was assisted into a wheel chair and was taken away for examination down one of those endless light green corridors which seem to characterise hospitals.

Shelagh and David went out to park the Land Rover and then returned in search of Eric. They found him alone in a waiting room. Jennifer had been taken for X rays and it would be a little while before the precise extent of her injuries were known. However, the doctor's initial diagnosis had been that, broken bones apart, she had come through her ordeal remarkably well. Eric said he would stay on; he felt that Jennifer needed someone there. She had been blaming herself for what had happened to Stuart and would want to know his position. She would also want someone to contact her parents and maybe others. He was happy to sit and read magazines meantime and would either phone David or make his own way to his house once he could no longer be of use. They left him there promising to phone later in the day.

It was still dark when they went out although there were some signs of life. David suggested to Shelagh that, in view of the time, she could come back with him for soup and a sandwich and that she could kip down in his spare room. He would take her back to Ambleside or Elterwater with the Land Rover later in the day. Shelagh looked at him consideringly for a moment and then said she would be glad to take him up on the offer. She got on the radio to Advanced Base to let Joe know that the casualties had been safely delivered to Hospital, that David would bring the vehicle back to Elterwater later in the day and that they could both be contacted on David's number if needed.

"That should raise some eyebrows," observed David.

Shelagh smiled.

Near Great Knott, 5.30am

The storm was still raging but it sounded as though the wind had dropped to a mere gale. Tom and Tania had been lying arm in arm contented and relaxed. Outside the wind was by no means spent. It still blew hard but it seemed as though the hurricane had passed.

"We should make a move," said Tania.

Tom got out his mobile and sent a text message to his Mum for onward transmission to Advanced Base to say they were on the move again. They shared a cup of coffee and had a bite to eat. Then Tom plotted their position from the GPS. This showed that they had about half a mile of gradual climbing before they could head down into Eskdale. Tania set a compass course. Then they packed their sacks and stuffed the bivouac bags away. With Tom holding the flashlight, they ventured out of their trench in the snow and out from behind the sheltering rocks. The wind still tore at them out of the darkness and the snow was still driving past but by putting their heads down they were able to make headway. Tania kept close behind Tom, following in his footsteps. Tom set a slow but steady pace as they worked their way slowly up the hillside.

Three times over the next half an hour Tom stopped so that they could check their progress against the map with the aid of the GPS. Their worry was that if they turned downhill too soon they would descend into Mosedale rather than Eskdale. On the third occasion they concluded that they could change the bearing and start heading downhill to cut across the line of Swinsty Gill which would take them down into Eskdale. Care would be needed because the map showed small cliffs across their path and they were thankful of the flashlight.

In fact, fortune smiled on them and steered them between the cliffs and after another half a mile of gradual down hill they came across a stream heading downhill in a westerly direction. A check with the GPS confirmed that this was Swinsty Gill and they adjusted their bearing again to take them down its left bank. At a suitably sheltered spot, Tania suggested that they should see if they could raise the Ravenglass Mountain Rescue Team who would be co-ordinating the rescue in Eskdale. She took out her radio.

"Ravenglass Control, Ravenglass Control, this is Langdale Tania, do you read, over?"

The radio crackled into life. "Langdale Tania, this is Ravenglass Control reading you strength 4. What is your position?"

Tania gave the grid reference.

"It's good to hear you. We were worried about you," said Ravenglass Control. "It will be another half an hour before we get to Brotherilkeld Farm and set up advanced Control. You will probably get to the party in Lingcove Beck before we do. They are sheltering in a ruined sheepfold. There should be three of them."

Control gave an approximate grid reference for the sheepfold. Tania asked Control if they would pass a message to Langdale Control to say they were descending into Eskdale and then signed off.

Tom and Tania continued on down beside the stream for about a thousand feet before reaching the junction with Lingcove Beck. Again, they checked their position with the GPS and adjusted the bearing to take them south west following the beck down the Eskdale Valley. For the first time in a long time the wind was now behind them.

"OK," said Tom looking at the map, "If the grid reference is accurate, it shouldn't be far now. We should come across the sheepfold within the next quarter of an hour." Although it was still dark, he noticed that the darkness was beginning to lighten a bit.

Brotherilkeld Farm, 6.30am

Lucy had been so wet and cold when she broke into the farmhouse that she had decided to have a bath. She had thought the occupants of the farm would understand and she thought she would probably just have time before the rescue team arrived. On investigation she had found that her luck had clearly changed at last because there was hot water in the tank. The occupants of the farmhouse apparently had not intended to be away for long.

Lucy had stripped off her wet clothes and looked with concern at her knees. They were gashed, bleeding, discoloured and swollen. Her elbows too were showing signs of wear and tear and her ankle was also bruised, swollen and angry looking. Lowering herself into the bath was an extremely painful business as first her ankle, then her knees and finally her elbows protested at the immersion in hot water. Once in she had been able to rest and had lain there for a while with her mind vacant and her cares soaking away. Her mind, however, had refused to remain vacant for long. Her conscience had insisted on reminding her that she had twice gone to sleep when she was supposed to be going for help. The consequences for her friends may have been fatal. She would find out soon enough. These thoughts had spoiled her bath and after gingerly trying to wash the worst of the dirt from her knees and elbows, she had eased herself out again and had sat on the edge while she dried herself with a borrowed towel. There was a dressing gown behind the door and she had put this on.

Having cleaned out the bath, she had hobbled off in search of a tumble drier to see if she could dry off some of her clothing before the rescue team turned up. She had found one in the utility room off the kitchen, had stuffed everything in but her waterproofs and had switched it on. Then she had gone back into the dining room and had cleaned up the glass from the broken window. She had wondered about finding something to block the window so as to prevent the snow from finding its way through but after a half hearted search she had been unable to come up with anything. Instead she had gone into the kitchen and made herself a mug of tea. Then she had found pen and paper and had written a note to the occupier explaining the circumstances, apologising for the damage and leaving her name and address. After that she had sat down in a comfy chair to finish her tea and had fallen asleep.

The strident ringing of the phone woke her with a jolt. It took her a moment to remember where she was. As she made her way with difficulty into the hall, she glanced at her watch and realised that she had been asleep for an hour and a half. There was still no sign of the rescue team.

"Hello," she said, "Brotherilkeld Farm."

"Hello," said a voice, "this is Sergeant Brian Ramsay of the Cumbria Police. I thought I should phone because I know you will be anxious about the length of time it is taking for the rescue team to arrive. I'm afraid the road up the valley is totally blocked and the helicopter can't fly in conditions like this. Although we have a snow plough clearing the road, it broke down for a while; so it may be another half an hour before we get through. But the rescue team are making their way up on foot and should be with you shortly. Are you OK?"

Lucy assured him she was fine and rang off. Then she made her way through to the utility room and found that her clothes had dried in the tumble drier. She struggled into them enjoying the warmth and returned the dressing gown to the bathroom. Her waterproofs were still damp but she packed them into her rucksack and left the sack with her boots beside the door. Then she sat down to wait for the team.

Sheepfold, 7.00am

Black night had definitely turned to grey dawn thought Tom; daylight must be coming. He could just see the outline of those rocks over there and he wouldn't have been able to do that half an hour ago. Suddenly he realised that the rocks formed a sort of wall and that that could well be the sheepfold. He shouted to Tania and pointed. She nodded and they made their way over. For a moment they thought no one was there. Then they realised they were looking at two snow covered bodies. They quickly cleared away the snow. The first appeared to be a large girl with her head tucked inside an orange bivouac bag. The second was a man lying in the open just in a shirt, although incongruously he was still wearing waterproof trousers.

They checked for vital signs. The man had none and they thought he was dead and had been for some time. Nonetheless, both Tom and Tania knew enough about hypothermia to know they should not assume this. The girl seemed more promising. They thought they could detect a very weak pulse and very shallow breathing; and her eyes responded to the flashlight. They were unable, however, to wake her.

"Right," said Tom. "Let's sort out our priorities. We seem to be missing one of the party, so can you make a quick check of the vicinity in case he is nearby. If he is not, can you let the rescue team know so they can mount a search. I'll see if I can insulate the man against further heat loss."

"OK," said Tania. "After that I'll see if I can get into the survival bag with the girl."

Tom took off his jacket and fleece and with some difficulty got the fleece onto Peter. It was probably a waste of time but they had to assume there was a chance until a medic told them otherwise. He then put his jacket back on and zipped it up tight around himself. He retrieved the survival bag from underneath Sam and after a struggle managed to get Peter into it to help insulate him from the cold. Then he got into his own bivouac bag and spread it around them both. Tania, meanwhile, after a brief but fruitless search of the immediate vicinity, got on the radio to report the contact and the condition of the party to Ravenglass Control. Predictably, they were worried by the missing third person.

"We have just arrived at Brotherilkeld Farm so we will send an advanced party to you with casualty bags and first aid for hypothermia," said Control. "Hopefully we will come across the third person along the way; but in case we don't, I will organise a sweep search along the valley as soon as we have enough people. Sit tight until we arrive. Out."

The priority in cases of severe hypothermia, such as Peter was exhibiting, was immediate evacuation but that would not be possible until the rescue team arrived with stretchers. As Peter was not breathing, Tom thought about commencing chest compressions and ventilation but rejected the idea. Present thinking was that this should only be started if it could be continued; an interruption could be harmful to the casualty. In this case resuscitation would be interrupted while Peter was evacuated to the farm by stretcher. In the meantime, the best Tom could do was to try and prevent him getting any colder. He remembered that in past times severely hypothermic patients were immersed in very hot baths - not that that was an option in this case. However research had shown that rapid external rewarming could trigger shock and raise the risk of heart attack.

Tania, meanwhile, made Samantha as comfortable as possible and ensured she was well insulated against the cold. She talked to the girl while she was doing this and tried asking her name but without any real hope of a response; and she got none. She did, however, discover that she was not dealing with a big girl as she had first thought; just a well-clothed one. It was clear now where the man's jumper and jacket had gone. She then spread her bivouac bag around the two of them and made herself as comfortable as she could using her rucksack as a pillow.

Tania and Samantha were lying beside Tom and Peter. Tom passed Tania the flashlight so she could brighten things up. Although it was getting a bit lighter outside, it was still quite dark under the bivouac bags.

"Do you want a drink or a bite to eat?" asked Tom. "I've got both in my sack."

Tania said she could manage a bit of both so they shared a cup of still warm coffee and Tania had some chocolate and nuts.

"You know, that was quite a walk we did," said Tania. "Conditions don't come any worse than that. I couldn't have managed it without you."

"Nor I you," said Tom simply.

"Did I see you taking off your fleece?" said Tania.

"Yes," said Tom.

"I know why you did it but I don't think that is very sensible. It won't help anyone if you go down with hypothermia," she said.

"It probably isn't sensible," agreed Tom, "but we have to give him every chance and there is really nothing else we can do for him. I'm not cold at the moment and if I start feeling it, I'll take it back. There are limits to my generosity."

Brotherilkeld Farm, 7am

Lucy's ordeal eventually finished just before 7am when an advanced party from the Ravenglass Rescue Team arrived at the farmhouse. Miles Dawson introduced himself as team leader. Lucy explained as best she could where the rest of the party would be found. Just then the message came in from Tania to say that they had found two of the party but that the third was missing. Lucy was unable to account for the third person but could only suggest that Adam had perhaps set off to get help in view of the length of time she had taken. Where he had got to was a mystery. Miles immediately dispatched four team members to follow the path up the valley with casualty bags and first aid gear and with instructions to keep an eye open for the third member of the party. Six others were sent on after them carrying the team's two stretchers.

Then, while Lucy was examined and her ankle and knees treated and bandaged, Miles took her slowly through her story. He was adept at spotting and probing any area of reticence and at the end of twenty minutes he was satisfied he had the whole story. He had been a mountaineer long enough to have a very good idea of what she had been through. She didn't seem much to look at; but her slight figure clearly belied her strength of will. He knew she would be worried about her friends and there was nothing at the moment he could do to alleviate that; but he thought there was probably something he could help with.

"I suspect you may be feeling guilty about the length of time it took to call us out," he said; "That's quite natural but you shouldn't be you know. Many people in your position would have given up when they damaged their ankle. To literally drag yourself along the valley like that in the middle of the night in a blizzard shows real determination. It's no surprise you flaked out at times; there is nothing you can do about exhaustion. You did very well. You have absolutely no reason to feel bad about it and, whatever the outcome, your group are lucky to have you. Now you just relax as far as you can and we will take it from here. I'm afraid you will have to repeat all this to the police when they arrive; but once we can get a vehicle up here we'll get you off to the hospital and you can get a proper rest."

"Thank you," said Lucy quietly, "you don't know how helpful that is. Incidentally, what about the house, the broken window, the use of the bath and so on."

"Oh don't you worry about that," said Miles. "The tenant is a good friend of the team and is coming up with the vehicles once the road is open. He should have been back last night but got stranded by the weather. He will be more than happy that his house was of help to you. And the police will sort out the window. Now you just try and get a bit of rest. You must be in need of it."

Lucy felt able to relax properly for the first time since the group had lost their way on Crinkle Crags. She drifted off into sleep while the rescue carried on around her.

The team vehicles got through to the farm about ten minutes later and Miles, with the help of his deputy, Alan, immediately set about organising a sweep search along the valley to try and find Adam. He reasoned that wherever Adam had got to he would probably have stayed down in the valley. Miles had eleven team members at his disposal and spread them evenly across the valley floor from the river to the start of the rising ground. One team member was tasked to make a careful visual check of the river itself. Miles reminded them to be careful to check any unevenness in the snow covered ground which might hide a person and to look closely at the base of walls and behind boulders where Adam might have taken shelter. As soon as the line was ready, it moved off into the still driving snow with Alan controlling it from the middle. Miles remained at the farm to run Control.

It was important if the sweep search was to be effective to try and keep the line together and as straight as possible. Once the line broke up, there could be no guarantee that all the ground had been searched. With the limited visibility due to the weather, Alan could only see the team members on either side of him so controlling the line was difficult; but all the team members had radios and GPS units, so he took it slowly and stopped the line every five minutes to check positions using the GPS units and to monitor ground coverage. Miles at Control made a note of the uphill extremity of the line at each check of the position. If they did not find Adam by the time they reached the ruined sheepfold, they would have to reverse the sweep and return along the slope of the valley and Miles would know what had been swept and what had not.

Sheepfold, 8.15am

"Happy New Year," shouted a voice.

Tania and Tom were jerked out of their reverie by the voice. Tania shrugged off the bivouac bag. Four snow encrusted figures were trying to tuck themselves into the limited shelter of the ruined sheepfold. One was on his radio to Control reporting their arrival.

"It's good to see you," said Tom emerging from his own bivouac bag.

The figure who had been on the radio introduced himself as Geoff Price and then introduced the other three. Tania introduced herself and Tom.

"OK" said Geoff, "what do we have?"

"This one is alive," said Tania pointing to Sam, "but suffering from hypothermia. She has a detectable pulse and is breathing; but we couldn't bring her round when we arrived. We have insulated her against the cold. We could probably try bringing her around now. The other one we found just in his shirt and without any vital signs. In the circumstances, we put him in a survival bag, Tom gave him his fleece and has made him comfortable."

"John, could you and Andy check out the other one. We will see what we can do with this one," said Geoff. "This must be Samantha."

"Sam, Sam," he said, " Can you hear me?"

There was no response and he repeated the question with his mouth close to her ear. This time he thought he detected a low groan.

"Let's see if we can get her to drink something," he said rummaging around in his rucksack. He poured some juice into a cup and, lifting Sam's head, put the cup to her lips.

"Sam, Sam see if you can drink something," he said tipping the cup so that the juice spilled across her face. Some went into her mouth and Sam choked and opened her eyes.

"Hello Sam," said Geoff, "do you think you can drink a bit of this; it will help to warm you up." The eyes were unresponsive.

"Sam, see if you can drink some of this; it's warm fruit juice," said Geoff again. This time Sam responded as he put the cup to her lips and she managed to swallow some, although quite a lot went down her neck.

"OK, that's good," said Geoff drying off her neck. He introduced himself and explained that he and the others had come to take her back to the farm where she could have a bath and something to eat and put on some dry clothes. He gave her some more to drink and this time Sam managed to swallow most of it.

"All right," said Geoff, "now we have this wonderful machine which provides warm air and that should help to stop you getting any colder. Will you give it a try?" he asked.

Sam nodded and one of the others extracted a warm air breather from his rucksack and held it while Sam inhaled.

Geoff had moved over to where John and Andy were kneeling beside Peter. John shook his head.

"Like a block of ice," he said. "Absolutely no sign of life. I think he has been gone sometime."

"OK," said Geoff. "Let's get him into one of the casualty bags."

Geoff got on the radio again and reported the condition of the casualties. Control said that stretchers were on their way.

Tania and Tom helped themselves to a hot drink from one of the other team members and Tom managed to get borrow a spare jumper which he put on.

Sam was clearly benefiting from the warm air apparatus and had taken a break from it while she took another warm drink and swallowed some glucose tablets. Tom and Tania also had a couple.

"How are the others?" asked Sam. It was the first thing she had said since she had come round.

Geoff said that Peter was unconscious and they needed to get him to the farm as quickly as they could. Lucy was all right. She had badly damaged her ankle going for help and had had to crawl to the farm on her hands and knees to call out the team but she was resting now. Adam had not turned up and the team were out looking for him between here and the farm.

Sam digested this in silence.

"Thank you for coming out to get us," she said eventually.

"That's OK," said Geoff. "I'm only sorry it took us so long to get here. We would have been here sooner but we had to wait for a snow plough to open the road and then the plough broke down. Incidentally, you should thank these two," he said pointing to Tania and Tom. "They got to you first. They came over the top from Langdale in some very nasty weather."

"Thank you," said Sam looking at the two of them. Tom looked sheepish while Tania smiled and said she was glad Sam was looking better.

Shortly after, the other team members arrived with the stretchers and Peter was immediately strapped on and six team members picked it up and set off on the return journey to the farm. Sam had a further period with the warm air breather and then Geoff judged that she was sufficiently recovered to be moved. She was tucked into a casualty bag with the warm air breather to hand and strapped onto the second stretcher. The remaining team members, including Tom and Tania, took their places around the stretcher and on Geoff's command they lifted it and set off after the others helped along by the wind which still howled down the valley.

Eskdale, 8.45am

It was slow work sweeping up the valley in limited visibility. The stretcher party carrying Peter emerged out of the driving snow and passed through the sweep line while the team worked its way forward. The stretcher party had been able to sledge the stretcher much of the way but had to carry it over rough terrain. After a sweep of about a mile, the valley narrowed considerably. Alan did not think there was much point in sweeping very far up the hillside at this stage and he reduced the length of the line. That in turn enabled him to speed up the sweep; the gap between team members was reduced and it took less time to check the ground.

Above the waterfalls just north of the junction between the River Esk and Lingcove Beck, the path up the valley climbs quite steeply until the way forward is blocked by a low cliff. The path skirts this to the right. Adam was found covered over in snow, lying behind a boulder not far from the bottom of the cliff.

Alan called everyone over while a paramedic in the team examined him. Adam had clearly received a nasty bang on the head but the paramedic did not think the skull was fractured. There was no other obvious indication of injuries; but he was very cold and there were no vital signs. The paramedic was surprised to find Adam was not wearing a jersey of any sort and that was quickly remedied and his jacket was exchanged for drier one.

"Right," said Alan. "We don't have a stretcher with us so I want him insulated from the ground and let's get him into a bivouac bag so he doesn't get any colder."

While this was being arranged, Alan got on the radio to Control and explained the position. Control said that the other stretcher party was on their way down and should be passing them at any time. Miles pointed out that they only had the one casualty bag and one stretcher, so one of the casualties would have to wait. He would have a word with Geoff to see whether Sam might have recovered enough to be rested while Adam was brought down in her place. If Alan could provide fresh stretcher bearers, that should speed up the evacuation of the other casualty and enable them to recover both as soon as possible.

Miles then had a word with Geoff Price, who was accompanying Sam, about her condition. Geoff recognised it was a difficult call. Sam was conscious, warm and in fairly dry clothes and seemed to be making a good recovery; but she had recently been unconscious, she had been out in appalling conditions for a long time and she still seemed to drift off into another world at times. Geoff's initial reaction was to give priority to Samantha who was alive rather than to Adam who was probably dead. He explained his misgivings to Control. Miles thought about it. He was aware that gentle handling is critical with hypothermic cases and that, normally, decanting a casualty in the middle of an evacuation is not good practice. However, he was also aware that speed of evacuation was vital with severely hypothermic cases such as Adam if they were to stand any chance. He told Geoff that he thought in the circumstances they should make the change. Geoff accepted this and said he would make the arrangements.

The team members sent forward by Alan in due course met up with the stretcher party sledging Samantha and helped to bring it down to Adam's position. Geoff explained the situation to Sam and said that it was important that Adam should receive attention as quickly as possible and that, as they didn't have enough stretchers to go round, would she mind resting for a bit while they took Adam down first. Sam was delighted to hear that Adam had been found and said she was more than happy to make way for him. Indeed, she felt she was recovered enough to walk down if they could take it slowly. Geoff was pleased she had recovered to such an extent and felt easier about the exchange. He went on to say, however, that it was probably not advisable for her to walk down in these conditions. He thought they would only have to wait an hour before the first stretcher party returned. In the meantime, they managed to find a sheltered spot below the cliff and arranged as comfortable and as insulated a bivouac as possible while the change over was made. Adam was loaded into the casualty bag and onto the stretcher and sent on his way with the remainder of the team while Geoff and the paramedic remained with Sam and she continued to use the warm air breather.

The team doctor had arrived and so had two ambulances by the time the first stretcher arrived back at the farm. Peter was quickly examined by the doctor and then removed from the casualty bag and loaded onto the ambulance stretcher and put into the ambulance. The ambulance immediately set off while the stretcher party and their relief turned round and set off back to collect Sam.

The stretcher party with Adam was about half an hour behind and

Adam was loaded into the second ambulance and that too departed immediately for hospital.

Geoff's estimate proved to be a little optimistic and it was after 11am when the stretcher party arrived back to collect Sam. By then she was dead. She had collapsed suddenly and nothing that Geoff and the paramedic attempted had been able to revive her. The storm which had blown for almost twenty four hours died with her. It was as though it had lingered just long enough to collect its last victim. The cloud lifted off the valley as the stretcher party carrying Sam made its way down to the farm and a pale sunlight shone on Bowfell and Crinkle Crags looking very alpine in their heavy coating of snow.

The Hot Pot, 5pm, 10th January

It was almost 5pm when David eventually finished his narrative. The restaurant had been quiet and they had been left undisturbed apart from the occasional replenishment of the coffee pot. Outside a grey afternoon had turned slowly into a black evening. A street light on the waterfront cast a reflection on the still water of the lake.

Gordon had been making extensive notes while David had been talking and now looked thoughtful.

"Quite a story," he eventually said. "That's been very helpful. I hadn't really understood just what is involved in a rescue. I can see, incidentally, that you would be well aware of the circumstances surrounding Jennifer's rescue. How do you come to know so much about what went on in Eskdale?"

"Well, as I had ended up with one of the team's Land Rovers with me at Windermere, Joe phoned me during the morning on New Year's Day to ask if I would mind driving round the coast road to Eskdale to collect Tom and Tania. Shelagh and I drove over and we had a long chat on the way back about what happened to them. They were equally keen to hear the circumstances of the earlier rescue."

"What I don't really understand," said Gordon, "is why these rescues have become an issue. I know the press have been careful to avoid coming out into the open with criticisms; but the innuendo is there. Normally, I would expect the press to be supportive of the volunteer rescue services. What has triggered the reaction in this case?"

"Well, it seems that Joe had a run in with a freelance reporter who was snooping around during the rescue", said David. "He happened to be in the valley when the helicopter came over and thought he might be able to get a scoop. He wanted to join Joe in Control while the search and rescue was in progress. Joe sent him away with a flea in his ear. Unfortunately, he didn't go far but waited until the team came down with Jennifer. He then mingled with the team members while they were having soup and sandwiches and, not surprisingly, picked up enough information to put together a fairly accurate picture of what had happened. It seems he misrepresented himself as in some way involved in the search. He also found out about the second search which at that point had only just started. He must have stayed with the story because he somehow discovered that Joe deployed the South Lakeland team on the wrong mountain. When he wrote up the story, he carefully avoided criticising Joe for this; but somewhere he had dug up the story of Joe's first search and rescue as team leader where he had four teams in the wrong place and he clearly enjoyed drawing parallels."

"He then seems to have gone round to Ravenglass to follow up the second rescue," continued David. "There he found out about the business of swapping Samantha for Adam on the stretcher. Nothing he said at any stage in his report was inaccurate; it was the spin he applied to it. Unfortunately, he seemed to be very good at syndicating the story – if that is the right expression – it was picked up quite widely and that triggered the editorials about the case for professional rescue teams. As far as I can judge, it seems to have been a case of spite. The journalist was annoyed that Joe put his nose out of joint and decided to take it out on the team leaders."

"Well, the damage has been done," said Gordon, "and I'm afraid the relatives of those who died may well try and make the most of it at the inquest."

"What will be their objective in doing so, do you suppose?" asked David.

"Difficult to say," replied Gordon. "They may simply want to find out why certain decisions were made. Alternatively, they may be hoping to pave the way for a negligence action against the team leaders, although I should be very surprised if they make any headway with that. Or they may genuinely believe that a professional service would be better and hope to promote enough interest in the case to call for a public inquiry into the present system."

"What we need to do," continued Gordon, "is to try and anticipate where the questions are going to be directed and what aspects of the rescues are going to come under scrutiny. We then need to ensure that the team witnesses are ready to deal with these matters."

"Oh, by the way," he added. "I think Eric is the person to give evidence about the call out – he was the one who phoned. He also got to know Stuart and Jennifer better than you. I still think you are too closely involved to represent the rescue teams; but you can certainly help me with the preparation and you can help out at the inquest."

They went on to discuss possible issues for a while longer and then worked out a plan of action for meeting with the potential witnesses during the two week period leading up to the inquest.

Chapter 6

The Inquest, Tuesday 24th January

The day of the inquest was dull and overcast. An inquest is held in public and the proceedings were scheduled to start at 10am. By 9.45am the hall was beginning to fill up. The hall was set out with rows of chairs. At the front of the hall facing the chairs was a table for the Coroner and somewhat to the side was another smaller table at which the witnesses would give evidence. Gordon and David were sitting with the two rescue team leaders, Joe and Miles, on the front row of the seats. Their other witnesses were distributed around the hall. At the other end of the front row sat two elderly couples they assumed were the parents of Peter and Samantha with their lawyer, a Mr Coleshill, from Manchester. David pointed out Lucy and Adam who were both in the second row, the former with crutches, the latter in a wheel chair. Jennifer was sitting further back also in a wheel chair and with her left arm in a sling and her left leg in plaster. Eric sat beside her. There was a middle aged couple sitting on the other side of her and David took them to be Stuart's parents. The hotel had thoughtfully provided microphones. At the request of representatives of the press, a further table was provided for their use at the back of the hall. Among them Joe could see Richard Hope, the journalist who had accosted him during the rescue.

The Coroner took his place at the top table five minutes before proceedings were due to start and laid out his papers. Gordon and David both knew him quite well. Richard Hammond was a local solicitor who was also Clerk to the Windermere Magistrates' Court.

At 10 o'clock the Coroner tapped on the table and announced that he was here to hold concurrent inquests into the deaths of three people during the weekend of 31st December and 1st January. Although the identity of the deceased had still to be established in evidence, this was not a matter about which there appeared to be any doubt so that he could say that the first inquest was into the death of Stuart Morris and the second was into the deaths of Peter Stansfield and Samantha Slater. He went on to say that he understood that the families of the deceased were present and he expressed his condolences at their loss. He hoped that the proceedings would not be too painful for them and that they would understand the benefits of having the facts established. As there appeared to be a certain amount of evidence which was common to all three deaths, he thought it made sense to run the two inquests concurrently.

With something of a change of tone, the Coroner went on to say that he had seen a certain amount of press coverage of the events of the weekend in question and he wanted to stress at the outset that this was not a court of law; nobody was on trial and he was not here to apportion guilt or blame. This was a fact finding inquiry directed at providing answers to four questions:

- the identity of the deceased;
- the place of their death;
- the time of their death; and
- how the deceased came by their death.

In the nature of things, he continued, it was the last question that was usually the most difficult to answer. The proceedings would be inquisitorial rather than adversarial. He would call the witnesses in turn and ask them to give their evidence on oath relevant to establishing the answers to these four questions. When they had given their evidence there would be an opportunity for those most closely concerned in the events to ask questions either directly or through their solicitor. However, he went on to stress that he would only entertain questions relevant to the four matters that he had to determine. At the conclusion of the proceedings, he said, he would give his verdict on these matters.

He then went through the list of witnesses and the order in which he intended to ask them to give their evidence. He also noted the parties who had legal representation.

The first witnesses were the parents of Stuart, Peter and Samantha who gave evidence as to identity. This was a straightforward if painful part of the proceedings. After that the witnesses were taken chronologically starting with Jennifer. She gave evidence in a quiet but clear voice about her relationship with Stuart and the events leading up to the accident on Hanging Knotts. She broke down in tears when she had to describe how her own slip had caused Stuart to fall to his death. The Coroner intervened to say that he realised how painful it must be to have to speak about this and that she should take her time. She went on in a firmer voice to speak about her actions after the accident leading up to the rescue. The

Coroner asked a question about her and Stuart's experience in winter conditions. No one else had any questions and the Coroner thanked her for her evidence.

Eric was the next to take the stand and he recounted the circumstances leading up to his telephone call to the police on the Saturday evening.

The Coroner then asked Joe to come forward. Joe's evidence took the story on from the time of the call-out to the organisation of the rescue, the bringing in of the helicopter, the finding of Stuart and his evacuation, and the search for Jennifer and her evacuation. He then went on to explain the circumstances of the second call out but the Coroner stopped him at that point and said it would make sense to deal with one rescue at a time and that he would recall him later to deal with his involvement in the second rescue. He also added that the inquest was not really concerned with the rescue of Jennifer but simply with the events up to the point where Stuart was evacuated by helicopter.

Alex took his place to give evidence about how Stuart was found and what happened after that. The Coroner asked about conditions on the hill and Alex said they were the worst he had experienced in all his time in the rescue team. Apart from the break of about two hours just before midnight, the wind was blowing a full gale from the north and it increased for a while to hurricane force sometime after they had evacuated Jennifer. Tania would be able to give evidence about that, he added. The combination of high winds, driving snow, cold and darkness made for very difficult conditions. Part of his concern that night had been to get team members off the hill as quickly as possible.

"Can you tell me something about the liaison between the team on the ground and the helicopter during the rescue," said the Coroner.

Alex described how pleased and surprised he had been to have the assistance of the helicopter that night. He went on to relate the sequence of events following the first appearance of the helicopter at Angle Tarn and concluded by describing how close the helicopter had come to disaster. He said he could well understand why the helicopter had had to withdraw; he was only glad it had been able to help at all.

Ben followed Alex to give evidence about his assessment of Stuart's condition. The Coroner noted that Ben had not pronounced Stuart dead at the scene of the accident. When the Coroner had finished, Gordon, knowing how important this point was likely to be with the second rescue, asked Ben what the normal practice was with casualties who exhibited no vital signs but who, like Stuart, had been out in the cold. Ben explained that there had been a few well-documented cases of mountaineers who appeared to have died from hypothermia but who had subsequently been revived. Although he had not been involved, he thought one of the casualties in the second rescue was a good example of this phenomenon. Hypothermia occurs, he went on, when the body's core temperature is lowered through exposure to the cold. It seems that, as a defence mechanism, the body closes down all unnecessary systems and concentrates on protecting the core. Because of that, rescue teams are unwilling to pronounce hypothermic casualties dead, even though they exhibit no vital signs, until they are warm. Indeed, the convention is to report them as having 'very weak vital signs'. Stuart had certainly been hypothermic, although he was also suffering from severe, almost certainly life threatening, injuries sustained in the fall. Time was clearly of the essence in such cases; if they were to stand any chance, the important thing was to evacuate the casualty as quickly as possible. In this case, he had been doubtful about the time lost in diverting the helicopter to look for Jennifer but he could understand why the decision had been taken.

When Gordon had finished, Coleshill asked whether, in Ben's experience, the same imperative of speed applied to conscious casualties suffering from hypothermia. Ben confirmed that, as a generalisation, it was important to get them down as quickly as possible. He added, however, that sometimes it was advisable to take time to warm up the casualty at the scene and to provide them with nourishment. That way they were better able to cope with the ordeal of evacuation; and sometimes after such treatment, hypothermic casualties even recovered to such an extent that they could walk down unaided rather than being carried.

Coleshill asked Ben whether he would agree that speed of evacuation was nonetheless the overriding objective in such cases.

"I wouldn't put it quite like that," replied Ben. "Speed is certainly important; obviously you are removing the casualty from the hostile environment which brought about the hypothermia in the first place. But there is a critical element of judgement here which has to be made by the person in charge at the scene. You have to weigh the benefits of speed of evacuation against the benefits of warming and nourishing the casualty. In my opinion, the benefits of the latter will quite often outweigh the former."

"But you are not saying," intervened the Coroner, "that time should have been taken to warm and nourish Mr Morris, are you?"

"No," said Ben, "with cold, unconscious casualties, like Mr Morris, time is of the essence."

Ben was followed by Flight Lieutenant Ron Corfield, the pilot of the helicopter, who explained their involvement in the rescue. He emphasised that conditions that night had been so bad that they had had only a small window of opportunity in which to operate.

"Is that why you were unable to assist on the second rescue," asked the Coroner.

"Yes, that is correct," replied Ron. "The blizzard returned just as we were reconnoitring the gully at the request of the leader on the ground". He went on to describe the sequence of events in the attempt to locate Jennifer in the gully. There were gasps from the public when he described in a matter of fact way how the ten tonne helicopter had been tossed by the wind towards the cliffs. He added that the blizzard had continued for the rest of the night and through to about 11 am the following morning so they had been unable to render any further assistance. They had simply uplifted the stretcher with Mr Morris and had delivered him to Lancaster Hospital and had then returned to base.

The Coroner asked whether the crew had worked with the Elterwater team before and, if so, what impression he had of the way in which the team operated.

Ron replied that he and his predecessors had worked with the Elterwater team for more than twenty five years. The relationship was a good one. They had always seemed to him very professional and that night was no exception.

The only remaining evidence on the first rescue was from the consultant at Lancaster Hospital who had attended Stuart and who confirmed he was dead on arrival and that death was probably caused by the injuries he sustained.

The Coroner at this stage said he thought this was a good time to adjourn the inquests for lunch. He indicated that he would start again at 2pm.

At 2 o'clock, Lucy came forward on crutches to give evidence about the disaster that had befallen the second party. She narrated how they had got lost when the blizzard closed in and how they had been uncertain where they were but eventually assumed they had come down into Eskdale. She painted a picture of the tiredness, uncertainty and anxiety that had affected the party. She described Peter's fall in the stream and their worry over his subsequent conduct. She explained why and how they had gone to ground in the sheepfold and how Samantha had also seemed to be suffering from exposure. Then she described how Adam had sent her for help, how she had subsequently broken her ankle and how this had significantly delayed the call out for which she blamed herself. She explained how she had eventually arrived at the farm only to find it empty and how finding that the public phone box had been vandalised had proved to be the last straw. She concluded by explaining how she had eventually returned to the farm house and had broken in to call the police and how she had then waited for the team.

It was clear that her narrative touched a sympathetic chord with the public and the Coroner felt constrained to comment that she had no cause to blame herself for delay. A broken ankle was an unfortunate accident, it immobilised most people and it was entirely to her credit that anyone in the party had been saved. She had shown very considerable determination. Lucy hobbled back to her seat in tears.

Lucy was followed to the stand by Adam who was rolled forward in his wheelchair by his mother. Adam's fingers and toes had been affected by frostbite and were swathed in bandages. He looked very pale.

He recounted how, after Lucy's departure from the sheepfold, he had done what little he could for Peter and had then got into the survival bag with Samantha to try and keep her warm. He had then waited in the sheepfold for hours for help to arrive with the storm raging around him. After several hours, he had been unable to detect any further signs of life in Peter and had assumed that he was dead. Samantha had also lapsed into a sort of stupor. Eventually, after more than seven hours, he had concluded that some accident must have befallen Lucy and he decided to go for help himself. He had managed to revive Samantha and had given her a drink and something to eat and had explained what he was going to do. He had dressed her in Peter's jacket and jumper and his own jumper and had put Peter's survival bag underneath her for insulation. Then he had set off during a lull in the storm. Unfortunately, the lull had proved to be short-lived and the storm had returned in its full force. He had lost touch with the river which he was trying to follow and that was the last he could remember until he came to in hospital.

Coleshill asked him on what basis he had assumed that Peter was dead. Adam said that Peter had stopped breathing and he could find no pulse. Coleshill asked him whether he had a first aid qualification and whether he knew how to check for signs of life. Adam acknowledged that he had no qualification and that he had never before had to check for signs of life; he had just done what he thought was best in the circumstances. His concern was that Samantha would also die and he wanted to give her the best chance of survival.

"Did you hear the evidence given this morning by Dr Benjamin Chapman about unconscious, hypothermic casualties?" asked Coleshill.

"Yes," answered Adam, "although I had not heard of this before."

"Even if you were correct about the lack of vital signs, it is entirely possible, is it not, that Mr Stansfield was not dead when you removed his clothing?"

There was silence for a moment and then Adam said: "Yes, I have to accept it is a possibility."

"It is also a possibility, is it not," continued Coleshill remorselessly, "that your actions in stripping the clothes and survival bag from Peter Stansfield caused his death?"

There was silence again and then Adam said in a low voice: "At the time I did what I thought was best. I thought Peter was dead and I thought I was giving Samantha a chance of life. If I had known then what I know now, I would not have done it."

There was silence in the hall.

Then the Coroner thanked him for his evidence and Adam was wheeled back to his place looking very stressed.

Joe then resumed the stand to give evidence about the circumstances surrounding the second call-out. He started with the report from the two men about the empty tent and went on to say that he had decided to respond to it, notwithstanding that the absence of the party might be explained by New Year revels, largely because the party had not removed the indecipherable note from the car windscreen. He described the difficulty in knowing where to focus his resources in the absence of any information about where the party had gone, except the assumption that they had started from Langdale. Having already covered all the main tracks at the west end of the valley on the first rescue, he went on to say that he had committed the South Lakeland team to checking the tracks on the equally popular north side of the valley. For completeness, he had also directed two of his own team, who had not been involved in the first rescue, to checking the path to Red Tarn. He added that he had then spoken to the team leaders or deputy team leaders of the Borrowdale and Ravenglass mountain rescue teams with a view to enlarging the area of search if nothing had been found by daylight.

He then went on to explain his actions following the call from the police which indicated that the party had in fact gone down into Eskdale. He only had two team members within reach of Eskdale and he had consulted with the team leader of the Ravenglass team, who would be taking control of the rescue, to see whether they could be of use. Following the consultation, he had asked Tania and Tom whether they could cross over into Eskdale and had asked the South Lakeland team, who were spread out on the north side of the Langdale valley to return to the New Dungeon Ghyll Hotel. That had effectively concluded his involvement with the second rescue.

When the Coroner had finished taking Joe through his evidence, Coleshill indicated that he had some questions.

"In view of the conditions that night, it was likely, was it not, that speed in locating the casualties was going to be of the utmost importance?"

"Yes," said Joe.

"And your decision to direct the South Lakeland team to the north side of the Langdale valley delayed the finding of the casualties by several hours, did it not?"

"I don't think so," responded Joe.

"Please explain yourself," said Coleshill.

"Well, Tom and Tania set out before the South Lakeland team and were already on their way up towards Red Tarn when they were diverted over to Eskdale. They were in fact already on the most direct route to Eskdale. I don't believe the casualties could have been found any quicker than they were."

"But if you had not directed the South Lakeland team to what turned out to be the wrong mountain, you would have had more resources at your disposal in Eskdale and it might have been possible to evacuate the casualties sooner," suggested Coleshill.

"Had I seriously thought at the outset that Eskdale was the most likely location, I would have explained this to the Ravenglass team leader, offered what help I could, and left it to him to decide how to recover them. It's his area. I doubt if I would have called in the South Lakeland team at all. But I had no reason at the outset to regard Eskdale as the most probable location."

"How often in your experience have parties on Crinkle Crags lost their way in bad weather and gone down into Eskdale?" asked Coleshill.

"From time to time," responded Joe. "But I had no basis for assuming they had gone up Crinkle Crags," said Joe.

"You are aware, are you not, that Mr Stansfield left a note of his proposed route on the windscreen of his car?" Coleshill asked Joe.

"Yes," said Joe. "Unfortunately, by the time it was recovered it was illegible."

"But it is correct isn't it that you were able to decipher the words crag, tarn and pike in that order?" suggested Coleshill.

"Well, we thought we could discern those words but the note was very smudged and we could not be sure," responded Joe.

"Knowing the Langdale valley as well as you do, is it correct that the most obvious combination involving those three names would be Crinkle Crags, Red Tarn and Pike O'Blisco?"

"Well, that is one combination," said Joe; "but it is not the only one; nor is it really the most obvious one. Tarn Crag, Stickle Tarn and the Langdale Pikes is perhaps a more obvious combination.

"It is correct, is it not, that the combination of Crinkle Crags, Red Tarn and Pike O'Blisco was suggested to you by one of the police officers during your initial discussion of the position?" said Coleshill.

"Yes, it is correct," responded Joe, "but that was only one of several permutations discussed at that time and, as I said, I did not regard it as the most obvious. In any event, given the illegibility of the note, I thought it unsafe to rely on guess work. On the basis of the search we had already conducted, it seemed to me that the north side of the valley would be the sensible place to start the search. That tied in with what I thought was the most likely interpretation of the note; but I have to say that, for the reasons I have given, I did not give the note much weight."

Joe was released at that point and his place was taken by Tania. David had wondered why Gordon had done his best to ensure that Tania rather than Tom would give evidence about their epic. Now it was obvious. He was playing a sexist card and David could see the impression she made on the public as she came forward. She was an attractive young woman who radiated health, fitness and confidence. One or two of the so-called 'gentlemen' of the press literally had their mouths hanging open. They had clearly categorised rescue team members as all beards and anoraks. Tania had even put on a smart two piece suit for the occasion. It was the first time David could remember seeing her legs he thought admiringly, falling headlong for the sexist card himself.

Rather like Jennifer before her, Tania spoke in a quiet yet clear voice. She described the instructions she and Tom had initially received from Joe, the subsequent request to divert over the top to Eskdale, the conditions they had encountered in doing so and the need to go to ground for a while because of them. Again, there were gasps from the public benches when she described how she had been literally blown off her feet by the force of the wind. The picture she painted in such a factual way of the two of them struggling across the mountains in the dark, in the driving snow, and in the storm force wind clearly made a tremendous impression on everyone in the hall. There were smiles when she explained how Tom had made use of his mum to keep people informed of their progress. She went on to describe their descent into Eskdale, how they had found the casualties, the condition in which they had been found and how one was missing. She concluded by giving details of how they had then attempted to give them warmth while waiting for the Ravenglass team to arrive.

There was silence when she finished. Coleshill clearly saw no mileage in attempting to question her. The Coroner simply thanked her for her evidence.

Then Miles Dawson took the stand. He took up the story from the point at which the Ravenglass team had been called out in response to the phone call from Lucy. He explained his frustration in finding that the road to Hard Knott Pass was blocked by snow and how, in the absence of a helicopter, there had been no alternative but to wait for it to be cleared by a plough; how the plough had then broken down causing further delay; how he had jumped at the news that two of the Elterwater team might be able to assist but how he had been concerned for them knowing the conditions they would be facing. He went on to explain how some of the team had eventually got to the point where they could go on ahead of the plough to establish contact with Lucy at the farm; and how he had been astonished at Lucy's tale of perseverance notwithstanding her broken ankle.

He described the radio exchange with Tania; how he had sent on an advance party with first aid kit, nourishment and casualty bags to the sheepfold followed by a party with the two stretchers; and how he had then organised a sweep search for Adam. He recounted the events at the sheepfold leading up to the evacuation by stretcher of both casualties, as recorded in the radio exchanges. He explained how the finding of Adam had presented him with a dilemma because he only had two stretchers available for the three casualties. As the party carrying Peter were already well on their way to the farm, he had had to choose whether to give priority to Adam or Samantha. He had received an account of Samantha's recovery and in the light of that he had given priority to Adam because, in Dr Chapman's terminology, he was cold and unconscious and required urgent evacuation. He had been shocked when Samantha had died while waiting to be evacuated.

Coleshill indicated that he had some questions.

"You knew, didn't you, that the call out involved three casualties?"

"Well, it was clear at the time of the call out that three people were missing", responded Miles. "By the time we arrived at the farm it was also clear that two were casualties. At that stage, the third person was simply missing," responded Miles.

"Did you expect to find him unharmed?" asked Coleshill.

"I was not optimistic," said Miles.

"In the circumstances, it would have been reasonable to assume that you might need three stretchers, would it not?" asked Coleshill.

"It was certainly possible we might have three carries to undertake during the course of the rescue. The expectation was, however, that they would not all have to be carried out at the same time so that we could manage by shuttling two stretchers."

"But your priority would be to evacuate the casualties as quickly as possible, would it not?"

"No," said Miles. "Not necessarily. As Dr Chapman pointed out earlier, with hypothermic casualties it is sometimes better to spend time warming and nourishing them before evacuating them. The information available to me suggested that Mr Stansfield would require immediate evacuation but that Ms Slater would need treatment on site."

"With hindsight, there is no doubt is there that you would have been better to have allocated three stretchers to the rescue?" said Coleshill "Had you done so, there would have been no need to decant Ms Slater and she might not have died."

"With hindsight, I accept that it would have been better to have allocated three stretchers to the task," said Miles; "but I did not have three at my disposal."

"Is it correct that if a hypothermic casualty is alive when found but dies during evacuation, he or she must have been subjected to inappropriate treatment by the rescuers?" suggested Coleshill.

"I would say that was too simplistic," responded Miles. "If the casualty is alive when found, I would agree that there should be a good chance of survival. But much will depend on weather conditions, the condition of the casualty, the terrain over which recovery has to take place and the equipment available to the rescuers."

"In the case of Ms Slater, I would accept that the weather was abominable," continued Coleshill. "But she herself had recovered consciousness and was even talking of walking down herself, the terrain was relatively straightforward and your equipment, apart from the lack of a stretcher, was good – was it not?"

"Yes," said Miles, "I would accept that. I would add, however, that if core body temperature is lowered, any casualty is at risk of cardiac arrest and this can happen at any time."

"Would I be correct in suggesting that gentle handling is critical with hypothermic casualties?" asked Coleshill.

"Yes," replied Miles.

"Would you say that decanting a casualty from a stretcher and removing her from a casualty bag, as happened in this case, amounted to gentle handling?"

"I believe the change over was handled gently," said Miles. "I would agree, however, that such changes should be avoided if possible."

Unfortunately, I had to make a decision and the choice I made involved change."

"In making that decision, you took advice from the person in charge of the recovery of Ms Slater did you not?" asked Coleshill.

"Yes."

"That was Mr Price, wasn't it?"

"Yes."

"Is it correct that Mr Price counselled against removing her from the stretcher? He felt she should be accorded priority."

"Yes," said Miles.

"Why did you disagree with the person at the incident. What further information did you have which gave you a better light on the matter?"

"I had no further information. I viewed the priorities differently to Geoff Price. Geoff was quite right to express his misgivings. There was a risk in moving Ms Slater. Equally there was a risk in not moving Mr Moore. I thought Ms Slater had recovered sufficiently to cope with a further delay. I thought Mr Moore required urgent evacuation."

"You accept that your decision to delay the evacuation of Ms Slater may have contributed to her death?"

"It is not certain, but I accept that may be the position," said Miles.

"If you had to make the decision again, would you alter the priorities, knowing what you now know."

There was silence in the hall while Miles thought about that. "I'm not sure," he said. "But, on balance, knowing what I now know, I think 'yes', I would probably have given Samantha priority."

"Thank you," said Coleshill.

Gordon indicated that he wished to ask a question.

"You have said in response to the question from Mr Coleshill that with hindsight you would probably have altered your decision about priorities. If I were to suggest to you that by giving Adam Moore priority, you saved his life, do you still say you would have altered your priorities?"

"Are you saying that one would have died and one would have survived whatever I had decided?" asked Miles.

"It is a possibility, isn't it?" asked Gordon. "What I am really putting to you is that, subject what the medical evidence may say, we really do not know what might or might not have happened if you had taken a different course of action. We don't know whether Adam Moore would have survived if his evacuation had been delayed; nor do we know whether Ms Slater would have died even if she had been given priority – do we?"

"No," said Miles.

"In this climate of uncertainty, someone had to make a decision on the information available and that someone was you as team leader, wasn't it?"

"Yes", said Miles.

"How many mountain rescues have you taken part over the years?"

"I don't know," replied Miles. Certainly more than two hundred."

"And how long have you been team leader of the Ravenglass team?"

"Five years," said Miles.

"Thank you," said Gordon.

The medical evidence followed. Peter had been pronounced dead from hypothermia on arrival at hospital. Adam had initially been thought to be dead but tests had shown a very low level of activity almost as though his body had gone into hibernation. He had been slowly warmed up and revived. The evidence had been unable to say how critical any further delay would have been; they could say with certainty that the longer the delay, the less chance he would have had.

The medical evidence on Samantha was equivocal. She had died from cardiac arrest probably as a result of the shock to her body from the conditions she had experienced. It was not possible to say whether her removal from the stretcher had aggravated her condition or whether it would have happened anyway.

That concluded the evidence. In view of the volume of evidence, the Coroner said he would adjourn for an hour to consider his verdict.

Gordon and David went through into the hotel lounge with Joe and Miles and ordered some coffee. Others from the inquest came through as well, including Eric and Jennifer with Stuart's father and Tania and Tom.

"How do you think it has gone?" said Tom to Gordon.

"Well, the Coroner has kept it tight and well focused. I should be surprised if there is anything unexpected in his verdict."

"Will he just answer the four questions he posed," asked Eric "or can he go on and make remarks about the rescue itself and some of the comments that have been made."

"Difficult to say," replied Gordon. "He will certainly try and provide answers to the four questions. Coroners do sometimes go on and comment on related matters; but I can't somehow see him entering into the debate about professional as opposed to volunteer rescue teams."

"How are you getting on," David asked Jennifer. When are you likely to be out of plaster?"

"It should be off in the next fortnight, all being well. Then it will be a question of physiotherapy to try and get the leg back to normal. I guess I'm lucky. I haven't really had a chance to thank the team for what they did," said Jennifer to Joe. "I really am truly grateful. Sitting there listening to the evidence made me realise how much I owe you."

"Me too," said Stuart's father. "Although Stuart didn't make it, I know you did your best in very difficult conditions. Your expedition across the top to Eskdale almost defies belief," he said looking across at Tania and Tom. "Certainly the gutsiest thing I have heard of for along time. I think all this nonsense in the press is outrageous."

Tom looked embarrassed. Tania said: "Thank you. Fortunately, we don't have to do that very often."

The talk turned to other rescues and then people started drifting back towards the hall. The Coroner reappeared prompt on the hour and re-opened the inquest.

"I said at the beginning that the purpose of these inquests was to try and answer four questions in respect of each of the deceased. Having heard all the evidence, I am in position to do so. I want to thank all those of you who have given evidence today. I realise what an ordeal it can be. Fatal accidents touch, not just the victims, but those involved in rendering assistance and the friends and relatives of the deceased. Accidents sometimes call for tough decisions to be made and we have to do our best when faced with them. No one can ask for more.

Having heard the evidence, I do not, for example, think Mr Adam Moore should feel in any way ashamed about his decision to remove clothing from a friend he thought was dead to give a chance of life to another friend who was still alive. I do not think Ms Lucy Croft should feel in any way guilty about the length of time it took to call out the rescue team.

Quite the contrary, I hope she will come to feel some pride in the quite astonishing determination she showed in making it through to the farm against such adversity. I have no doubt that Mr Moore owes his life to her. I do not think there is any cause for criticism of Mr Joe Henton's decision to focus the rescue effort initially on searching the hills on the north side of the Langdale valley; it would seem to me on the evidence to have been the logical next step. Nor do I think Mr Miles Dawson should reproach himself for the decision he made about giving priority on the stretcher to Mr Moore rather than Ms Slater. He had a difficult decision to make, only he could make it and it was not one he made lightly. I hope he will be able to take comfort from the almost miraculous survival of Mr Moore. It is all too easy to criticise with the benefit of hindsight. I can well understand that, with hindsight, all these people might have decided to do things differently; but we are not blessed with hindsight and they had to do the best they could with the information available to them at the time. Nothing I have heard today leads me to believe that they did other than their best."

With regard to the four questions, I find that Stuart Morris died through misadventure on Bowfell on the night of December 31st/ January 1st. The time of death cannot be given with any greater precision. I find that Peter Stansfield died through misadventure in Eskdale on the night of December 31st /1st January. Again it is not possible to be more precise about the time. And I find that Samantha Slater also died through misadventure in Eskdale at around 10.30 am on 1st January. I should like to extend my sympathy again to the family and friends of the deceased."

"There is one further matter on which I wish to comment. I am aware that the circumstances surrounding these deaths have provoked considerable discussion in the media and even controversy. Arguments have been traded about the advantages and disadvantages of professional as opposed to volunteer rescue teams. These are not arguments in which I can or should involve myself. I do, however, think it is entirely appropriate for me to say on the evidence that I think we were very well served by our rescue teams on this occasion. We have much to be thankful for that they are willing to turn out to help their fellow beings in such atrocious conditions. I was much taken with Flight Lieutenant Corfield's assessment of the Elterwater team, and he is a professional, that in his opinion the team are always professional; and from what I have heard it would seem to me that the same comment could be applied to the Ravenglass team. The journey we heard about made by Ms Phillips and her companion over the mountains at night time in the teeth of the storm to assist a party in distress seems to me to epitomise all that is best in our present system and we can be thankful for it."

"That concludes the inquests."

This time it was not just her 'companion' who was embarrassed. Tania had the grace to go bright red as well.

Angle Tarn, May 28th, 12 noon

Angle Tarn and Hanging Knotts Crag sparkled in the summer sunshine. The four of them sat quietly eating their packed lunch. Occasionally a party passed by on the track leading to Esk Hawse but they were alone by the tarn.

Jennifer had recovered from her injuries. Indeed, it was the mental rather than the physical anguish that had caused her the most difficulty. She would never quite get over the fact that it was her slip that had knocked Stuart to his death; but she was beginning to see things in perspective and to accept that mountaineering can be dangerous and that accidents sometimes happen. Stuart's father had been a great help to her. When she had been at her lowest, she had gone to see him as a sort of expiation to say how sorry she was for what had happened. He had not put her off with platitudes. Instead, he had said that he missed Stuart terribly and would give a great deal to be able to turn the clock back. He talked a lot about him that afternoon and Jennifer had been quite frank about the nature of their relationship such as it was.

"You know," he had said as she was leaving, "Stuart thought a lot of you. That may surprise you because he was never very demonstrative; but he wrote about you in his last letters. I know the relationship did not have time to develop and with his impatience it might have come to nothing. But I am glad he found you. It's a comfort to me that he could be so discerning. I wanted to say thank you to you for being with him."

Subsequently, he had written to her to say that he had thought about making a donation to the rescue team – to help it maintain its 'volunteer' status – and wondered whether she would like to be associated with it. She had been only too pleased to be involved even though that particular debate about the status of rescue teams had died down as quickly as it had blown up. The Coroner's concluding remarks had seen to that.

Now she had come back to the scene of the accident. She couldn't explain it but she felt she could not go forward until she had first gone back. It was a form of pilgrimage. She had come up with Eric who had been such an undemanding support to her over the months since the accident and they had stayed at David's flat. It was a Bank Holiday weekend and Shelagh had come over and they had had a surprisingly lively evening. David hadn't seen Jennifer since the inquest but she turned out to be good company.

They had driven up to Langdale in the morning and had followed the path taken by Stuart and Jennifer up the Band and onto Bowfell. From there they had made their way to the top of Hanging Knotts Crag and Jennifer was able to see where they had gone wrong in the blizzard. After that they went down through the Ore Gap to Angle Tarn for lunch. It had been a quiet expedition; they had left Jennifer alone with her thoughts.

Indeed, David had been deep in his own. He had been thinking how strange it was that the same storm, which had so tragically destroyed three relationships, had also created three more. His own relationship with Shelagh had developed steadily since she had stayed the night following the rescue. They had discovered that they had more in common than a shared love of the mountains and that had provided a foundation on which to build.

The relationship between Tom and Tania had endured. David had realised when he had driven over with Shelagh to collect Tom and Tania from Eskdale on New Year's Day that their experience had created a bond between them. That did not surprise him; but it was only later that he realised the nature of the bond. Shelagh and Tania were close friends and through that friendship he came to know Tom much better in the months that followed the rescue. Together, he and Shelagh were able to put together a picture of what had happened during the night of the storm. The relationship had matured Tom. He was more confident in himself, less awkward in company. Tania too had benefited. She was more at ease with herself and with others, less distant than she had seemed before.

Of course, these relationships had not escaped the notice of other team members and they had become the subject of much gossip and speculation.

Greg had even suggested that the team should be renamed the Elterwater Dating Agency.

The third and in some ways the most surprising relationship to emerge from the storm was that between Eric and Jennifer. David knew at the time that Eric had felt protective towards Jennifer but he had attributed that to a natural feeling of sympathy for the victim of an accident. By the end of the New Year break, he realised that there was more to it than that. He saw little of Eric in the months that followed but he heard that he had continued to see Jennifer and it was clear that he had developed an affection for her. David was surprised, however, when Eric had phoned to arrange this weekend. He had not realised that his feelings had developed so far and he had no idea whether they were reciprocated. It was a relief to find that they were. David was worried that Stuart's ghost might forever bar the way to her affections. That had worried Eric also; but Jennifer had been quite open with him about her relationship with Stuart. While there was an enduring feeling of guilt that she had not given more of herself to him, particularly on that last night, she was sensible enough to acknowledge that they had actually never been more than good friends. Eric's support during her long process of recuperation had clearly forged a strong attachment between them.

Jennifer had not known how she would feel when she saw the gully again; it had dominated her mind for so long. But in fact, she saw it for what it was: just an ordinary and undistinguished gully on the side of one of Lakeland's more popular mountains. It was a bit of an anti climax. But it was also a release and she was able to ask questions about the rescue and the three of them found themselves describing in detail both the drama and the drudgery of that night.

The weather, however, this summer afternoon was infectious. The hills looked friendly rather than forbidding and Angle Tarn was invitingly blue green in the sunshine.

"How about a quick swim?" said Eric.

"That sounds like a good idea," said Jennifer.

Odd Corners in Appleby, Gareth Hayes
(£8.50, ISBN 1 9045240 0 1)

The Ghastlies, Trix Jones and Shane Surgey
(£3.99, ISBN 1 9045240 4 4)

Changing the Face of Carlisle, The Life and Times of Percy Dalton, City Engineer and Surveyor, 1926-1949, Marie K. Dickens
(£8, ISBN 0 9540711 9 0)

From Clogs and Wellies to Shiny Shoes, A Windermere Lad's Memories of South Lakeland, Miles R. M. Bolton
(£12.50, ISBN 1 9045240 2 8)

A History of Kaber,
Helen McDonald and Christine Dowson,
(£8, ISBN 0 9540711 6 6)

The Gifkin Gofkins, Irene Brenan
(£2.50, ISBN 1 9045240 1 X)

A Dream Come True, the Life and Times of a Lake District National Park Ranger, David Birkett
(£5.50, ISBN 0 9540711 5 8)

Gone to Blazes, Life as a Cumbrian Fireman, David Stubbings
(£9.95, ISBN 0 9540711 4 X)

Changing Times, The Millennium Story of Bolton, Barbara Cotton
(£12.50, ISBN 0 9540711 3 1)

Better by Far a Cumberland Hussar, A History of the Westmorland and Cumberland Yeomanry, Colin Bardgett
(Hardback, £26.95, ISBN 0 9540711 2 3)
(Paperback, £16.95, ISBN 0 9540711 1 5)

Northern Warrior, the Story of Sir Andreas de Harcla,
Adrian Rogan
(£8.95, ISBN 0 9523282 8 3)

A Riot of Thorn & Leaf, Dulcie Matthews
(£7.95, ISBN 0 9540711 0 7)

A Country Doctor, Dr. Isaac Bainbridge,
Dawn Robertson
(£2.25, ISBN 0 9523282 32)

Military Mountaineering, A History of Services Expeditions, 1945-2000,
Retd. SAS Major Bronco Lane
(Hardback, £25.95, ISBN 0 9523282 1 6)
(Paperback, £17.95, ISBN 0 9523282 6 7)

Yows & Cows, A Bit of Westmorland Wit,
Mike Sanderson
(£7.95, ISBN 0 9523282 0 8)

Riding the Stang, Dawn Robertson
(£9.99, ISBN 0 9523282 2 4)

Secrets and Legends of Old Westmorland,
Peter Koronka and Dawn Robertson
(Hardback, £17.95, ISBN 0 9523282 4 0)
(Paperback, £11.95, ISBN 0 9523282 9 1)

The Irish Influence, Migrant Workers in Northern England,
Harold Slight
(£4.95, 0 9523282 5 9)

Soldiers and Sherpas, A Taste for Adventure, Brummie Stokes.
(£19.95, 0 9541551 0 6)

North Country Tapestry, Sylvia Mary McCosh
(£10, 0 9518690 0 0)

Between Two Gardens, The Diary of two Border Gardens,
Sylvia Mary McCosh
(£5.95, 0 9008111 7 X)

Dacre Castle, A short history of the Castle and the Dacre Family,
E. H. A. Stretton
(£5.50, 0 9518690 1 9)

You can order any of our books by writing to:
Hayloft Publishing,
South Stainmore, Kirkby Stephen,
Cumbria, CA17 4EU, UK.
Please enclose a cheque plus £2 for UK postage and packing.
or telephone: +44 (0)17683) 42300
For more information see: www.hayloft.org.uk